DEMOB

DEMOB

by
KENNETH HARPER

Adapted from an original script by
Dean Lemmon and Andrew Montgomery

YORKSHIRE
TELEVISION

First published in Great Britain in 1993 by
PAVILION BOOKS LIMITED
26 Upper Ground, London SE1 9PD

Designed by John Youé

A CIP catalogue record for this book is available from the British Library.

ISBN 1 85793 210 2

Printed and bound by Butler & Tanner, Frome

10 9 8 7 6 5 4 3 2 1

This book may be ordered by post direct from the publisher.
Please contact the Marketing Department. But try your bookshop first.

Affectionately and respectfully dedicated to

Les Dawson

A man of infinite jest.

CHAPTER 1

March,1946.

It was their last mission. Somewhere in England, two soldiers crept furtively along in the moonlight as a stiff breeze plucked at their khaki uniforms. They were on a dangerous assignment that called for skill and daring. This was to be a decisive strike against their greatest enemy.

Crouching low, they paused at the base of the tower to make sure that they were unobserved. Clouds drifted across the moon and they were wrapped in darkness. It was a good omen. They went up the vertical ladder with the agility of monkeys and reached the tank. The moon was again a willing accomplice, pushing aside the cloud cover to send down just enough light to illumine their target area. Lance-Corporal Ian Deasey and Private Dick Dobson wasted no time. They were professionals.

Their voices were crisp, hushed, conspiratorial.

'OK?' Ian asked.

'OK,' confirmed Dick.

'Let's get on with it.' He held out a hand. 'Charge,' he demanded.

'Charge.'

Ian took the small package from his companion and fixed it expertly to the steel valve with some tape. After testing his handiwork, he whispered another command.

'Detonator.'

'Detonator.'

Dick passed it over and watched with admiration as his colleague attached it to the charge. They had been on dozens of missions before but this one had special significance for both of them. Excitement shone in their eyes.

'Timer.'

'Timer.'

Ian Deasey held the last vital piece of equipment and scrutinized the dial. He was a man in his mid-thirties with the air of a perpetual schoolboy. Close-cropped black hair topped a long, oval face which could radiate manic delight and which in repose expressed a lugubrious good humour. He was a soldier with the features of a clown. Dick Dobson was younger, slimmer and more poised, with a shock of fair hair that swept back from a high forehead. He was debonair and carefully turned out and the educated drawl of his voice came in sharp contrast to Ian's pronounced east London accent.

The timer was set in position. Ian flicked back a cuff.

'Synchronize watches . . . '

'Twenty-two-oh-five,' said Dick, checking his own watch.

'Twenty-two-oh-five.'

A switch was flicked and there was a reassuring tick. The two friends exchanged a silent grin of congratulation. Everything had gone to plan.

The Naafi was ablaze with light and throbbing with noise. Hundreds of concerts had been held in the canteen at Stanhope Army Camp to raise the morale of the troops, but this entertainment was an important act of celebration. Next day, the men were due to be demobbed. An impromptu party was the ideal way for the drunken squaddies to laugh themselves out of their National Service. The Naafi was packed. NCOs and even a few junior officers had come along to join in the fun. The large room was pulsing with camaraderie.

Scott and Hodges stood on the makeshift stage and went through their routine with dismal eagerness. As second lieutenants, Scott and Hodges were amiable and fresh-faced young men: as a comedy duo, they were pure disaster. Lady Macbeth would have got more laughs. The audience were beginning to get restless.

The comedians surged on regardless. Dressed in a major's uniform, Hodges looked on in horror as food was ladled all over him by his partner. Scott wore a chef's white apron and hat. He dipped his ladle into a large urn and brought out some more dumplings. Ignoring the yelled suggestions of where he should put them, he slopped them on to Hodges's trousers.

'What do you think you're doing?' said Hodges.

'Giving you some Horses' Doovers!' said Scott.

'Horses' Doovers? Don't you mean, *hors d'oeuvres*?'

'No, I mean Horses' Doovers?'

Hodges strained a non-existent joke to breaking-point.

'Why do you mean Horses' Doovers?' he pressed.

'Because it's a la cart!'

They paused for a laugh but were met instead by a disbelieving silence. Scott and Hodges were about as comical as an air raid warning. The squaddies just gaped. One person appreciated them, however, and cut through the stillness with a hearty laugh. The audience groaned. If Regimental Sergeant-Major Quinn thought the act was funny, it must be even worse than they thought. Some of them began to slink mutinously out of the canteen. The two young officers went grinding on unmercifully.

When Ian Deasey and Dick Dobson entered, they took in the situation at a glance. The concert was on the verge of collapse. It was the men's last night, and they were being presented with a dismal leaving present. And there, sitting in the middle of it all, perched high above the rest, was the person who symbolized everything that was wrong with the British Army – Regimental Sergeant-Major Quinn. His back was straight, his uniform impeccable. A swagger stick rested across his knees. Ian and Dick bristled. RSM Quinn had made the last four years an absolute hell for them. He was now spoiling their farewell concert.

Scott and Hodges were still scraping the barrel.

'Look at this!' wailed Hodges. 'My uniform's ruined!'

'This bit isn't,' said Scott, finding a clean segment on which to daub some more stew. 'Now sprint across to the Officers' Mess. You can be their running buffet.'

Ian and Dick had endured enough. They moved quickly to the stage and jumped up to usher the two men off it.

'Thank you, thank you,' said Ian, taking charge. 'A big hand for Second Lieutenants Scott and Hodges, please. So talented and so brave . . . '

Jeers went up and a smattering of relieved applause broke out. The ordeal was over. Floundering amateurs had just been replaced by two men with a professional touch. Dick lowered himself on to the stool at the battered piano and played a few chords. Ian reeled off some quick-fire gags at the expense of the departing act. The mood brightened at once and those about to leave now resumed their seats with a hopeful smile. Their concert might yet be saved.

Ian Deasey came alive in front of an audience. He was a natural performer with a timing that Hodges and Scott could never attain. Having reminded them how to laugh again, Ian held up his hands to quell the noise.

'Now, settle down, lads. Or I'll bring Hott and Scodges back on.' Roars of amused protest. 'Hey, do you know, there's something happening tomorrow but I'm blowed if I can remember what it is . . . ' He scratched his head and let them jog his memory with yelled advice. 'Yes – *that's* it! We're going to be demobbed! The prison gates open. We'll be free!'

Shouts of approval came from everyone except the man in the very middle of the room. Regimental Sergeant-Major Quinn looked as though he were carved out of solid ice. A thin-faced Scotsman, he glared at Ian with a hatred that had built up steadily over four long and unforgiving years.

'We go home to a land fit for heroes!' said Ian. 'I'll be heart-broken to leave. There's a lump in my throat and an even bigger one in my trousers . . . ' Ribald laughter. 'But before we say our last farewells, it's only right that we should pay tribute to the man who saw us through the dark days in the desert. Without whom we would never have gained our crushing victory over the dastardly Hun . . . '

Right on cue, Dick began to play the chords of a march. His touch was light and the music had a mocking tone. Ian pointed at the object of his scorn.

'I mean, of course, Regimental Sergeant-Major Quinn!'

Hoots of derision and moans of pain went up as the men let Quinn know what they really felt about him. The Scotsman remained impassive amid the hostility. Ian spoke with heavy irony.

'RSM Quinn,' he continued, 'is the very quintessence of military discipline. A man of whom Rudyard Kipling once wrote – "He was a regular soldier, as regular as clockwork." In fact . . . ' He winked across at Dick. ' . . . you could set your watch by him.'

Quinn was assaulted by more catcalls but his gaze never left Ian Deasey, who continued to wreak his revenge.

'With luck,' he concluded, 'we shall not see his like again.' The loudest cheer yet went up. 'And so . . . '

Dick's deft fingers modulated the march into a tune that they all recognized. The words of 'Goodbye' however, had been rewritten by the two friends to suit the needs of the moment. They plunged in with well-rehearsed precision, each taking a line before singing in unison.

'My heart is broken,
But what care I?
Such pride inside us has woken
We'll try our best not to cry by and by
When the final farewells must be spoken
We've done our bit now, we've won the war.
Don't need to take any orders now,
Because tomorrow night for sure,
We won't be r-r-r-rankers any more!'

The audience roared its appreciation as Quinn suffered on. He was not yet out of the firing line. Ian's reedy tenor merged with Dick's slightly deeper voice as they took aim.

'For dear Regimental Sergeant-Major Quinn
We've all done our best,
Been true to the Red, White and Blue,
We've been digging khazis, fighting Nazis,
Eye-ties and the rest,
But now we've got sod all to do!'

When they reached the end, Ian and Dick were joined by the gleeful voices of their comrades as they took their leave of the British Army and the Regimental Sergeant-Major.

'Goodbye-ee, goodbye-ee!
We wish you all a last goodbye-ee!'

A resounding cheer went up from the happy men. Their concert had been rescued and their tyrant ridiculed. A whole new world awaited them tomorrow. They were now in the right frame of mind to greet it.

Deasey and Dobson were heroes.

☆ ☆ ☆

Stanhope Camp was up at the crack of dawn. For once in their lives, the men ate a nauseating Naafi breakfast with enthusiasm, then they raced across to the Quartermaster's Stores to join the queue for civilian issue. Long racks of hideous, badly cut two-piece suits stood ready. The storeman was handing them out at speed. Under the eagle eye of RSM Quinn, the line was kept moving.

Ian Deasey took his turn. Like the others, he wore only shorts and singlet. He handed back his neatly-folded uniform and smiled at the storeman.

'Give me something in tropical lightweight,' he said. 'I live in Walthamstow.'

The storeman looked him up and down with disdain.

'Thirty-eight chest. Herring-bone. Two-piece. Grey.'

'Grey?' complained Ian, turning to Dick Dobson. 'Do you see me in grey, Richard?'

'Not with your eyes,' said Dick, clicking his tongue. 'No, Ian. You need more of a beige.'

'Got a sort of bloodshot beige?' asked Ian.

But the storeman had already yanked a crumpled suit off the nearest rail and he flung it down unceremoniously on the counter. Ian grimaced and felt the material critically.

'Nothing in cashmere?' he asked.

'Next!' yelled the storeman.

'But I can't wear this.'

'Next!'

'You haven't even measured my inside leg.'

RSM Quinn moved in sharply. 'I'll measure the inside of your arse with the toe of my boot if you don't shift!' he barked nastily. 'Out!'

Ian Deasey nodded cheerfully and moved on. When Dick Dobson had been issued with an identical suit, he joined his friend. They went back to their Nissen hut to change and to laugh at each other's appearance. The suits were dreadful. Ian looked like a well-dressed scarecrow and Dick like a badly-dressed insurance agent. When they put on a trilby apiece, they both looked like derelict spies.

They were soon standing in another queue. Behind a table, an officious NCO was handing over documents to each man who came before him. RSM Quinn glowered in the background. His lip curled as he saw Ian Deasey step forward.

'Ration book, travel warrant, five pounds,' said the NCO briskly, handing them over. He thrust a book and a pen under Ian's nose. 'Sign here.'

'Five pounds!' Ian regarded the money with disgust. 'Four years of blood, sweat and tears for a fiver!'

'The rest is in your Post Office account.'

'I don't have a Post Office account.'

'Then it's at your home,' said RSM Quinn, intervening once more and putting his face inches away from Ian's. 'Get a bloody move on, *Mister* Deasey! The milkman's sneaking out of your back door and Mrs Deasey is lying naked on the bed. Panting, desperate, waiting for you . . . '

'I'll be off then,' said Ian chirpily, signing his name and picking up the documents. 'Cheerio, *Mister* Quinn. Give my best to Mrs Quinn and the quintets.'

'Sod off, Deasey, you little shit!'

'Thank you very much.'

Ian walked breezily out of Quinn's clutches for ever.

Half an hour later, he and Dick Dobson were part of the buoyant crowd milling about on the platform at Stanhope Station. All that the squaddies had was a fiver apiece in the pocket of their shapeless suits but they felt rich and happy.

Dick and Ian sipped from mugs of tepid tea and wondered about the future. Their close friendship had helped them to survive the rigours of war but all that was over now. What did real life hold for them? They were both uncertain.

The station announcer's voice boomed like a foghorn.

'Train for London approaching Platform Two . . . '

A cheer rang out and most of the men grabbed their kitbags and clattered across the bridge to the other platform. The train came steaming into the station. Ian Deasey was about to join the charge when Dick Dobson plucked at his sleeve.

'Hold on,' he said.

Ian hesitated. 'What?'

'Well. Four years. Been through a lot together.'

'So?'

'It's just that . . . we may never see each other again.'

'What do you want?' said Ian. 'A kiss?'

'No – the fiver you owe me.'

Their laughter eased the feeling of awkwardness.

'Keep in touch,' said Dick.

'I'll write twice a day,' promised Ian, running up the stairs with the stragglers. 'Enjoy yourself at Rugby!'

'Give my best wishes to Walthamstow!'

Ian raced on to the other platform and dived into the nearest compartment. Leaning out of the open window, he bellowed at Dick Dobson.

'Oi, fishface! Wearing that suit for a bet?'

Dick smoothed his lapels and tried to look affronted.

'This is a Deepcrotch and Chafe.'

'Ah yes. I know them well.'

A whistle blew and the engine started to belch steam. Accompanied by cheers from the opposite platform, the train pulled slowly out. Ian yelled a frantic goodbye to his pal then snapped back the brim of his trilby and pulled a funny face. Dick did the same, poking out his tongue and waving until the train had vanished from sight. He then heaved a sigh of regret.

Regimental Sergeant-Major Quinn marched angrily across the parade ground with a copy of the *Daily Mail* tucked under his arm. He had enjoyed wielding a cruel power over the men and felt cheated by their departure. But the life of a regular soldier had to go on. Ten o'clock meant a visit to the latrines.

Quinn went into the ramshackle building and past three empty cubicles with a measured step. Entering the fourth, he locked the door, lowered his trousers, sat down and studied the picture of the king and queen on the front page. He could almost hear the national anthem playing quietly in his ears. It was suddenly replaced by another melody.

'BOOOOOOM!'

The controlled explosion blew off the emergency valve on the water tank. Thousands of gallons began a headlong descent into the drainage system. Quinn was momentarily aware of the unearthly sound of fifty yards of raw sewage being forced back towards him at massive pressure. It surged out malevolently from the three unoccupied pedestals then met resistance in the fourth. A volcano erupted below Regimental Sergeant-Major Quinn and lifted him feet first into the air before depositing him in a mound of evil-smelling lava.

'Shit!' he roared.

He was – as always – right.

Deasey and Dobson had stolen the last laugh.

CHAPTER 2

Walthamstow had changed. The Luftwaffe had extensively remodelled the housing and done some drastic landscape gardening. A barrage balloon called Bertha still hovered above the Recreation Ground. Everything looked drab and neglected. Ian Deasey did not recognize the area. A US Army jeep had given him a lift from the station and dropped him off near his old street. He could not resist taking a nostalgic peep. It was a mistake.

'Bloody hell!' he murmured.

His little terraced house was now a pile of rubble. A direct hit had flattened it and left a gaping hole in an otherwise untouched row. Why had Adolf singled him out? It was unfair. The Deasey residence was like a missing tooth in a full set of choppers. His old life was buried for ever.

He turned quickly away and pulled out the scrap of paper on which his new address was scribbled. Ten minutes later, he was turning into Rosendale Road and searching for a number. A clutch of ugly prefabs had been thrown up on a patch of waste ground. The four-room bungalows were nothing more than jerry-built, tumbledown shacks.

Was one of these asbestos monstrosities his home?

Ian came to a prefab that was decorated with flags and bunting. There was a crude banner above the door – 'WELCOME HOME, OUR HERO!' His spirits were rekindled. With his kitbag over his shoulder, he went up to the front door and knocked. It was flung open by a small, snotty-nosed boy, who eyed him with deep suspicion.

Could this really be the loving son of a war hero?

'Yes?' grunted the boy.

'Alan?' said Ian tentatively.

'No.'

'You're not Alan Deasey?'

'Why? What's he done?'

'Don't know. I'm his Dad.'

'You want next door then.'

As the front door was shut, Ian looked at the neighbouring prefab. His heart sank. It was another Nissen hut. He put on a brave face and picked his way through the mud to knock on the door. A woman soon appeared, winding a towel around her wet hair to form a turban and mumbling an apology. Ian grinned inanely.

'Janet!'

'Ian! Oh, my God! Ian!'

They stared open-mouthed at each other for a moment then he dropped his kitbag and held her tight in his arms.

'I expected to see you tomorrow,' she said.

'You will.' He giggled. 'And today.'

'Alan's at school. He so wanted to be here for this.'

'I went to the wrong house.'

'You've come to the right one now.'

Janet Deasey was an attractive, shapely woman in her early thirties with sparkling eyes and a bright smile. Even with a towel covering her fair hair, she looked very pretty. Ian had forgotten how beautiful her complexion was and stared at her in wonder. She whisked him inside the house and shut the door. They embraced again and burst into wild laughter.

'What do you think of this place?' she said.

'We always wanted a detached house.'

'It was all they had, Ian.'

'Better than a wigwam.'

They giggled stupidly at each other then Janet took him through into the tiny living room. All their furniture had been destroyed by the bomb. In its place, they now had a grotesque sofa and two armchairs that did not match. Janet had found new ornaments for the mantelpiece and added other homely touches in the hope of creating an illusion of continuity. She saw herself in the mirror and shrieked with embarrassment. When she had dried her hair and brushed it out, she let him take a proper look at her. Ian beamed proudly.

There was so much catching-up to do that the hours flitted past. They were still trading news when they heard the thump of someone falling over Ian's kitbag in the hall.

'That'll be your son,' said Janet.

Ian got nervously to his feet, not knowing how the lad would react to him after a four-year absence. He was now a stranger in his own home. Alan Deasey was a thin, watchful boy of thirteen in blazer, short trousers and school cap. He came into the room with his grandmother, Edith Cooper, an alert and well-preserved woman in her sixties. Father and son stared at each other for a second then Edith nudged the boy and he held up a large sign.

It read 'L.N.E.R. – STRICTLY NO TRESPASSING'.

Ian was baffled. Alan realized his mistake and turned the sign over. On its reverse side he had painted the spidery legend – 'WELCOME HOME, DAD!'

No words were needed. Ian went to hug his son, then he gave his mother-in-law an affectionate peck on the cheek. Janet joined them in a communal embrace. Laughter mingled with tears and Ian Deasey was content.

He was back in the bosom of his family.

Dick Dobson was having second thoughts about returning to his own home. Having got as far as Rugby, he settled into the bar at the Station Hotel and ordered a series of stiff whiskies. Evening found him propped up against the public telephone. Pretending to be still at the barracks, he made his call short and sweet.

'Hello?' he said into the mouthpiece. 'Christabel? It's Richard . . . Yes, I'm in the pink, thanks. How's Brian? . . . Good. Listen, could you let my father know that I'm going to be delayed for a bit? It seems that the army can't manage without me.' He sipped from his glass. 'Oh, I don't know exactly. A couple of weeks at least. I'll be in touch. Bless you. Look forward to seeing you – *all* of you . . . '

Having bought himself more time, Dick put down the receiver and sighed with relief. He drained his glass before offering it to the barman. The latter shook his head solemnly.

'Almost closing time, sir.'

'But you're open to residents.'

'Yes, sir.'

'Check if there's a room free,' said Dick affably. 'Then I'll have the same again, please. I deserve it.'

☆ ☆ ☆

Alan Deasey was delighted with the sweets and chocolate that his father brought back in his kitbag, but he was less than pleased to be booted out of the house. Telling him that his parents needed to be alone, Edith manhandled him through the door with a promise that it was only for one night. Alan – 'Gerroff, Gran! Stop pushing me!' – was a reluctant evacuee.

Ian and Janet were left alone in the half-dark of the hall. He felt suddenly shy. He had often dreamed about this moment but, now that it had come, now that his rich fantasies could turn to reality, he was strangely bashful.

'Where's the . . . uh . . . ?'

Janet pointed to a door and he went into the bathroom. By the time he had cleaned his teeth and rejoined her, she was lying in bed in her nightgown with the sheets drawn up. They were both self-conscious. By the dull glow of the bedside lamp, Ian began to undo the buttons on his shirt. Janet did not know whether to watch him or turn away.

'There's new pyjamas in the second drawer,' she said.

'Ta.' He took them out and nodded. 'Very smart.'

When Ian hooked his thumb in the waistband of his underpants, Janet lost her nerve and averted her gaze.

'The old stag at bay!' he observed.

'What?'

'The Monarch of the Glen.' He pointed to the framed picture on the wall above her head. The noble beast gazed down at them from his crag. 'They didn't get him then?'

'No. Sole survivor of the bomb.'

Ian put on his striped pyjamas and climbed gingerly into bed. It was like their first night all over again and he tried to remember what he had done on that occasion.

'I've missed you,' she whispered, snuggling up to him.

'I've missed *you*, love.'

'How much?'

'Switch off the light and I'll show you.'

So she did.

Demobilization was delicious. Ian Deasey started to feel like a human being again. After a night of madness in his wife's arms, he brought her breakfast in bed. All shyness between them had disappeared and they teased and tickled each other like children. The only awkward moment was when Alan walked in to find his parents, helpless with mirth, rolling about on the bed together. They leapt guiltily apart. When Alan went off to school, however, the giggles continued.

Janet Deasey had another treat in store for him.

'I don't believe it!' he exclaimed.

'We knew you'd be pleased.'

'It's still in one piece!'

She had opened the door of their little garage to reveal Ian's motorcycle and sidecar. It gleamed almost as much as its delighted owner.

'Alan polished it religiously,' she said.

'What – every Sunday?'

She punched him playfully. Janet looked quite sporty in her ATS overalls and Ian wore his greatcoat and balaclava. They wheeled the machine into the road then he pulled down his goggles. Mounting the saddle, he attempted to kick-start the motorbike but all he got out of it was an apologetic gurgle. Janet moved him aside and took over.

'You need to tickle it up,' she said, giving the carb a tweak and twisting the throttle. A sharp jab of her foot brought the engine to life. 'There you go – Easey-Deasey!'

'You should see what I can do with a camel.'

'No thanks. Hop on!'

Ian was amazed. '*You're* going to drive?'

'Of course. Hold tight.'

He sat on the pillion with his arms around her waist. There was a roar of power and the machine shot away as if it were leaving the starting-grid in the Isle of Man TT Races.

Janet dropped her husband at the council offices, a large Victorian building whose echoing corridors stank of cheap disinfectant. Ian Deasey knew that smell of old and recoiled in disgust. Before the Germans had rearranged his career plans, he had passed all his working life in that grim, humourless cavern. Being back inside it was eerie.

Ian went up the staircase and along the corridor to the office of F W Parsons, Borough Engineer. He paused to smarten himself up and polish his shoes on the inside of his trouser legs. Frank Parsons was a stickler for appearances.

Taking a deep breath, Ian knocked loudly on the door.

'Come!' ordered a voice from within.

He entered the room, knowing exactly what his old boss

would say. Frank Parsons did not disappoint him. Taking a gold watch from the pocket of his waistcoat, the Borough Engineer checked it against the clock on the wall.

'What sort of time do you call this, Deasey?'

'Better late than never, Mr Parsons,' said Ian, smiling weakly at the heavy-handed honour.

'I suppose it is. Good to have you back.'

'Thank you, sir.'

Frank Parsons was a tall, cadaverous man in his sixties with a dark grey suit that fitted him like a pipe-cleaner. Though he tried to be genial, he always sounded faintly macabre. He rose to his feet to survey the newcomer.

'Army had enough of you, eh?'

'The feeling was mutual.'

'Was it?' He lowered his voice. 'Er, what exactly did you *do* in the Army? If it isn't classified, that is.'

'Oh, it was totally unclassified,' said Ian. 'Jerry always knew what we were doing before *we* did.'

Parsons gave a hollow laugh. 'So what sort of skills did you pick up? Training and that.'

'I dug holes in the sand.'

'Sand?'

'Sometimes in the mud.'

'Mud?'

'And I blew things up,' said Ian.

'Yes.' Another laugh. 'Very funny.'

'That's about it.'

'You blew things up?'

'Bit of fun, really.'

'Yes, well, Deasey,' said the other, becoming serious. 'While you were having a bit of fun in the desert, Jerry was having a whale of a time over here.'

'Of course. I'm sorry.' He manufactured a willing smile. 'I'm sure I can brush up on my old skills.'

'June!' Parsons called into the next office, then rubbed his chin thoughtfully. 'Blowing things up, eh? Demolition is Norman's department. You remember Norman?'

Ian groaned inwardly. 'How could I forget!'

A young woman marched in from the next office and Parsons ordered a cup of tea for his visitor.

'Milk and sugar?' she asked.

'Please,' said Ian.

'There isn't any sugar.'

'Er, June,' said Parsons, 'I wouldn't mind another – '

'You've already had two this morning,' scolded the secretary, heading for the door. 'Excuse me.'

Parsons gave a sigh of resignation then nodded to Ian. 'Let's meet the troops.'

Ian followed his boss along the corridor and into a gloomy office that was filled with gloomy people. They looked up from behind the mounds of paper on their desks and gave a deferential nod to their boss. Parsons struck a pose to make his speech.

'Your attention, please,' he called. 'Some of you may remember him, but for those who don't, this is Ian Deasey. He's just been demobbed after four years in the desert, fighting for King and Country. Ian's a bloody hero, and he's going to show us what hard work's all about. Starting 8.30 prompt. Monday morning.'

The clerks gave Ian a half-hearted round of applause and he shifted his feet in embarrassment. Five minutes in the building had already crushed his spirits. Did he really want to come back to this dreadful, dull, soul-destroying existence?

The secretary bustled in and handed Ian his tea.

'We found your old cup,' she said. 'In Sanitation.'

Dick Dobson had his best night's sleep in years, waking refreshed and ready to start a new life. He felt supremely lucky and he put that feeling to the test on a morning train to London, joining a group of demobbed soldiers in a card game and relieving them of every penny they had. When the irate losers saw him off at Euston with a fusillade of swear-words, Dick decided he had been down among the squaddies too long. It was time to promote himself to the officer class.

'Will that be all, sir?' said the man obsequiously.

'For the moment,' said Dick, admiring himself in the full-length mirror. 'What's the damage?'

'Here's your bill, sir.'

Dick had always wanted to go to a Savile Row tailor and he now understood why. Even off the peg, his new suit had a cut and elegance that marked him out as a man of distinction.

The regimental tie completed the translation of Richard Dobson, Private (Ret'd) to a higher and worthier rank. After preening himself once more in the mirror, he paid the bill with some crisp fivers and moved off with suave assurance.

'Wait,' said the man. 'What shall I do with this, sir?'

He was holding up the discarded demob suit. Dick turned to look at the last, miserable relic of his dreary days in the army. The herring-bone suit was the uniform of failure.

'Burn it,' he said with lordly contempt. 'Then scatter the ashes in a rubbish dump. Thank you, my good man . . . '

With a spring in his step, he headed for Piccadilly and was delighted with the respectful nods and admiring glances that he collected on the way. By the time he reached the Allied Officers' Club near Pall Mall, he was basking in his new-found self-esteem. Dick Dobson was going up in the world.

The Allied Officers' Club had the down-at-heel dignity of a requisitioned hotel. Dick went up the marble steps and into the lobby. Uniforms of half-a-dozen different nations could be seen moving about and snatches of Polish, French and Serbo-Croat could be heard amid the nasal English drone and the brash American drawl. Dick strode across to the desk and spoke to the club steward in a New Zealand accent.

'Good morning,' he said.

'May I help you, sir?' asked the steward.

'I was wondering if you could offer me a room.'

'Are you a member, sir?'

'Not as yet.'

'Then we'll require a reference.'

'Naturally,' said Dick with a winning smile. 'I was recommended by a chum – Wing-Commander Garton, Royal New Zealand Air Force. Old Garters speaks very highly of me.'

'Pardon me, old boy,' interrupted a clipped voice at his shoulder. 'Anything for me, John?'

'Yes, Major Lorimer,' said the steward.

He reached under the desk for a large parcel. Major Lorimer was tall, upright figure in his late forties with a moustache and thinning hair. He looked resplendent in his uniform and had the unmistakable habit of command. He exchanged a polite nod with Dick then took the parcel and stepped away to examine it. The steward turned once more to the visitor.

'Can I see your papers, please, sir?'

'Ah, well,' said Dick, 'that's the problem, you see. I've been robbed. Everything was taken except the clothes I stand up in. They've promised replacements but you know how it is. Bloody red tape.'

He lied with such confidence that the steward was taken in but Major Lorimer was less easily fooled. He glanced at Dick Dobson again then smiled quietly to himself.

In the kitchenette of their prefab, the Deasey family sat down for their evening meal. Ian forked a piece of meat into his mouth and munched it appreciatively.

'This is good,' he said. 'What is it?'

'Lamb chop,' said Janet. 'Enjoy it while you can.'

The delicacy had been her leaving-present from the other women at the motor pool where she had worked. In the belief that a man needed building up, the girls had put all their food coupons together to buy a single chop from the butcher. Janet had been touched by the act of sacrifice. She could give her husband a decent meal before rationing forced her back on the horrors of snoek.

'How was Frank Parsons?' she asked.

'Same as usual,' muttered Ian.

'What did he say?'

'Same as usual.'

'When do you start back?'

'Monday morning,' said Ian grimly. 'Same as usual.'

Alan Deasey wanted to hear tales of wartime heroism.

'What was the desert like, Dad?' he asked.

'Very hot,' said Ian. 'Lots of sand. Like Bournemouth.'

'Did you kill any Germans?'

'No,' he admitted, 'but I did once get very angry with one of them.'

Dick was enjoying his role as Squadron-Leader Dobson so much that he had almost come to believe in it himself. At the Allied Officers' Club that evening, however, the high flier ran into some heavy flak when he was accosted by a fellow-officer from the Royal New Zealand Air Force. Hearing the Antipodean twang, he pounced on Dick gratefully.

'At last! Another Kiwi!' he said. 'James Capel.'

'Dick Dobson,' said the other uneasily.

'You must have been up at Duxworth.'

'Well, yes and no . . . '

'Nothing to beat our Air Force, is there, mate?'

'No, no. Nothing at all.'

'You must've known old Boomer Bowman.'

'Yes,' said Dick with a forced laugh. 'Old Boomer, eh? How's the old bastard getting along.'

'Well, not too hot. He got shot down over Dresden.'

Dick swallowed hard and was wondering how he could talk himself out of the hole when Major Lorimer came strolling across the lobby with his friend, Colonel Palliser. They had heard enough.

'Squadron-Leader Dobson!' hailed Lorimer, taking his arm to shepherd him away. 'Do excuse me, but we'll be late for our appointment if we don't get a move on.'

The three men came out of the club and went down the steps. Lorimer and Palliser were both in uniform, Dick was still in his Savile Row suit. He beamed gratefully.

'Thanks, Major Lorimer,' he said. 'You're a pal.'

'I think we can dispense with the accent now,' said Palliser, a short, stout, middle-aged man. 'Don't you, *Mister* Dobson?'

'Oh, right,' said Dick in his normal voice, falling in beside them as they strolled off. 'Where are we going?'

'Well, *we're* going to a club,' said Lorimer.

'Mind if I sort of tag along?'

Dick Dobson tagged along all the way to Soho then he followed them down a flight of rickety stairs into a club with the unequivocal name of Les Girls. Dark, dirty and filled with raucous servicemen, it was the seediest night-spot in town. They brushed their way through curtains of tobacco smoke and went up to the bar. Lorimer confronted the proprietor, Constantine Costas, a fat and oleaginous man in a flashy dinner jacket.

Lorimer's brisk politeness turned to an overt sneer.

'This place is a pigsty!' he complained. 'I bring my friends like Squadron-Leader Dobson here, and they're in danger of catching fleas from your filthy customers.'

Dick Dobson heard no more because someone thrust a glass of whisky into his hand and the band took his attention to the stage at the far end of the room. The dancing girls came on to riotous applause and moved sinuously to the music. Their skimpy costumes had the men baying and drooling. The star was undoubtedly Hedda, a gorgeous, lithe young woman, who moved with the grace of a real dancer. Her body was so enticing that one of soldiers climbed drunkenly over the footlights and tried to grab her, only to be kicked neatly under the chin and sent sprawling into the arms of his mates.

Hedda did all it with great style and composure but her boss was furious. Costas charged towards the stage.

'Who does that snooty cow think she is?' he complained. 'Marlene Dietrich? She's got to stop kicking the customers.'

Lorimer finished his free drink and called to Dick.

'Come on, Dobbo. Let's get out of this stinking wop toilet.'

But Dick Dobson did not hear him. The dancers were leaving the stage and the next act was coming on. He could not believe his eyes when he saw the two fresh-faced men in matching loud-check suits and sensational ties.

'Good evening!' said one. 'I'm Tommy.'

'And I'm Jerry,' said the other.

It was Scott and Hodges. The comic catastrophes.

Dick was absolutely thunder-struck.

CHAPTER 3

Monday morning found Ian Deasey in disconsolate mood. He walked towards the council offices through the drizzle of Walthamstow and wondered why he did not feel more cheerful. He had survived the war in one piece and returned to a warm welcome from a loving wife and a growing son. Yet it was somehow not enough. The joy of seeing them again was offset by the humiliation of living in the prefab, a home with such paper-thin walls that privacy was impossible. Especially if you slept in a bed that creaked dramatically as soon as you even looked at it. Something was missing from Ian's life.

He had no hopes of finding it at his place of work.

'If it isn't deadly Deasey!'

'Ah. Hello, Norman. How are you?'

'Couldn't be better. Couldn't be better.'

'Good.'

'You look lost, old son.'

'I suppose I am, yes. Just a bit.'

'Follow me.'

Norman was the last person he had wanted to meet on his first day back. The man's enthusiasm was so lowering. Norman was a big, bluff man of his own age with fatal self-importance. Ian resented him before the war, despised him during it, and loathed him now that he saw that smirking face once more. Norman led him up the stairs, into the main office and across to a desk in the far corner. The other clerks gave polite nods of acknowledgement to their superior, who walked blithely past them as he threw questions over his shoulder.

'How's the wife? Janet, is it?'

'Very well, thank you,' said Ian.

'And the boy? What's his name?'

'Alan. He's very well, too.'

'I've got seven now, you know,' boasted the other. 'Three boys and four girls.'

'You've been busy Norman – those blackouts, probably.'

'My wife hated them. She's the nervous type.'

'So you couldn't leave her alone.'

They reached a desk which was groaning beneath sheaves of papers. Ian assessed the weeks of work that would be entailed to get through even half of them. He shuddered.

'Frank Parsons will keep you at it,' said Norman. 'Do you know how many homes we've lost in Walthamstow?'

'I suspect that you're going to tell me.'

'Eight hundred and forty-seven.'

'Give or take the odd privy.'

'Give or take the odd privy!' repeated Norman with a chuckle. 'You're a caution, you are, Deasey. A proper comic.'

'Thank you.'

His colleague's voice took on a confiding tone.

'Do you know something?'

'What?'

'I reckon . . .' Norman inflated his chest. 'I reckon that in six years, I could be deputy borough surveyor – if I play my cards right. Just think, Deasey. I'd have letters after my name. DBS.'

'Daft bloody sod!' said Ian under his breath.

'Deputy Borough Surveyor!'

'I'm impressed, Norman.'

'I've put in the hours,' said the other, defensively. 'You've been away, remember.'

'That's right. There was a war.'

'I couldn't go, you know. Not with my asthma.' He tapped his chest and wheezed pitifully. 'But I've got on.'

'You've done well, Norman.'

'I have, I have.'

He wandered off in a cloud of self-congratulation and Ian Deasey was left to contemplate his own situation. He took off the coat of his demob suit, draped it over the back of his chair then sat down at his desk. Piles of paper towered like slagheaps over him. Drudgery beckoned.

Was it for *this* he had faced danger in foreign climes?

He began to miss Dick Dobson.

☆ ☆ ☆

Life at the Allied Officers' Club suited Dick Dobson to perfection. His room was comfortable, his food excellent and his new friends remarkably obliging. He was moving among a different class of people now. Dick sat at the grand piano in the empty lounge, playing wartime melodies. As he lazily smoked a cigarette, he mused on the wisdom of his decision to come to London instead of going home. His fingers moved smoothly over the keys and the strains of 'We'll Gather Lilacs' wafted across the room.

Major Lorimer swept in from the lobby and paused to listen. He looked sleek and prosperous in a cashmere coat. He wore gloves but carried his hat. Lorimer gave an approving nod then stepped forward into Dick's line of vision.

'Very nice.'

'Good morning,' said Dick.

'Are you fit?'

'Absolutely!'

'Right. Let's go, then!'

'Lead the way!'

Dick got up from the piano and extinguished his cigarette in a glass ashtray. Gathering up his coat and hat, he followed Lorimer out into the lobby where the club steward was waving a piece of paper in the air.

'Squadron-Leader Dobson!' he called.

'Yes?' said Dick, changing his accent.

'Sorry to bother you, sir. But we do require you to fill out a registration form to stay here.'

'Catch me when I'm not so busy.'

Dick gave him a cheery grin then went out into the street behind Lorimer. The two of them joined Colonel Palliser, who was waiting for them beside a gaudy limousine that could only have been built in America. Dick whistled.

'This your car?' he said. 'Very smart.'

Lorimer smiled. 'Don't you think it's a bit showy and vulgar for these austere times?' he asked.

'Yes. That's what I like about it.'

'Would you like to drive?'

'Me?' said Dick in surprise.

'Why not?' He opened the driver's door. 'Get in.'

Dick obeyed and saw the key in the ignition. While he settled in behind the wheel, the others, in high spirits, got into the rear of the car. They were obviously relishing some private joke.

'Chocks away!' said Lorimer.

'Right.' Dick started the engine. 'Where to, gents?'

'Drop us off at the Waldorf.'

'Your wish is my command.'

'Then I've got some errands for you, Dobbin.'

Lorimer nudged the smirking Palliser and the two of them shook uncontrollably with mirth. Dick was puzzled but he took it all in good spirit. The men had introduced him to a new and exciting world. He was profoundly grateful.

The drive to the Waldorf gave him the chance to see just how much London had suffered during the war. Decay and debris were everywhere. Bombed sites littered some of the main thoroughfares and acres of scaffolding were being used to prop up damaged buildings. There were plenty of taxis about along with the occasional Austin, Ford and Standard, but there was nothing to compare with the ostentatious vehicle that he was now driving. People pointed and gaped.

If only Ian Deasey could see his old pal now.

It was evening by the time he reached the quiet square in Belgravia. Most of the day had been taken up with ferrying Lorimer and Palliser from one luxury hotel to another. He had now been given another task and pulled the car to a halt outside a beautiful Regency house with a marble portico. Taking a parcel from the back seat, Dick went up to the front door and rang the bell. It opened an inch and dark eyes peered out at him.

'Good evening!' he said. 'I have a delivery for —'

'Round the back!' snapped a voice.

The door closed abruptly. Dick shrugged and went around to the rear of the premises. It was far less prepossessing than the front and there was a rat-faced man waiting for him. When Dick offered the parcel, he snatched it from him and thrust a thick envelope into the courier's hand before vanishing back into the house without a word. It was quite mystifying. Dick's curiosity got the better of him and he crept up to a window in which a light was shining. When he bent over to peep in, however, someone tapped on his shoulder and he jumped back in alarm.

It was the same man. He had a simple message.

'Get lost, ponce!'

Dick Dobson went off to pick up his friends once more and parked the car outside Les Girls Night-club. Located in a narrow back street, its exterior was even more squalid and disreputable than its interior. He was kept waiting for a long time. The fat envelope lay beside him on the passenger seat, almost daring him to open it. Finally Dick succumbed to the temptation.

Breaking the seal with care, he glanced at the contents and gulped in amazement. He was holding a large wad of English pound notes. Noises from the club alerted him and he was just in time to re-seal the envelope before Lorimer and Palliser climbed into the rear of the car. Dick started the engine and drove off.

Rudi Lorimer could read his chauffeur's mind.

'Red Cross parcels, Richard,' he explained. 'That's what you are delivering. We are doing our bit for refugees. We have come to an agreement with the good Mister Costas. There will be a pick-up from his club tomorrow. OK?'

'OK.'

Lorimer felt generous. 'You can take some of what you found in that envelope, for your efforts.'

'Right,' said Dick. 'How much is "some"?'

Alan Deasey had gone down to the canal first thing on Saturday morning. He chose his spot on the bank, fixed his bait and cast the line. His fishing tackle was rudimentary but he had the concentration of a professional. He was still staring into the murky water when his father came strolling along. One glance told Ian that it would be a sticky conversation. He and Alan had just not managed to hit it off as yet.

'Morning,' said Ian.

All he got in return was a curt nod.

'Any luck?'

Alan shook his head. Ian sat down beside him.

'What bait are you using?'

'Bread.'

'Tried maggots?'

'Are they any good?'

'They're more difficult to butter.' He saw the ghost of a smile on Alan's lips and pressed on. 'I had this mate in the

Army. We used to sit in the rotten desert, talking for hours on end about fishing.' He sniffed. 'Mind you, he was more of a dry fly guy.'

'Where is he now?'

'Working on his father's farm, probably.'

Alan turned to look at him properly for the first time. 'What was it *really* like?' he pressed.

'Boring. Sometimes terrifying. And then boring again.'

'Is that all?'

The boy's face clouded with disappointment. He wanted a war hero. Ian was letting him down. It was time to fall back on one of his comic routines. Alan needed cheering up.

'There was one time,' recalled Ian, 'I had to take on a German panzer single-handed.'

'Go on.'

'We were pinned down outside Tobruk.' Ian acted out the scene with graphic gestures. 'I was separated from the troop. I'd been doing dangerous sabotage work behind enemy lines – turning the signs round, putting drawing pins on chairs, letting down the tyres on tanks. Anyway, I came round the corner of this wadi – that's a kind of public toilet used by the Bedouin tribesmen . . . '

'Like a khazi?'

'Yes, but much bigger. So they can get the camels in.'

'And?'

'There it was.'

'What?'

'This tank. Rommel's personal tank, I later discovered. The turret slowly rotated in my direction. Luckily, I had a sink-plunger in my pack. We all carried them, just in case.'

'Is that all you did?' said Alan dully. 'Tell jokes?'

'Well, sometimes people laughed.' He wanted to put an arm around his son's shoulders but somehow could not. 'I had what they call a good war, Alan.'

'What does that mean?'

'Well, I didn't get killed, for a start. I did what I had to do. I didn't let my mates down. Nothing else mattered to me.' He gave a shrug. 'Now it's over.'

Alan stared into the water as he thought it through.

'Let's go home,' he said.

It was a long and depressing walk back. Ian made a few

desultory attempts to draw Alan into conversation but all to no avail. They had lapsed into a deep silence by the time they turned into their road. Then they saw something which gave them both back their voices.

'Good God!' exclaimed Ian.

'Look at that car!' said Alan, pointing his rod.

The limousine was parked outside their prefab and Dick Dobson was peering in through their front window. In those bleak surroundings, an American car and a man in a Savile Row suit were totally incongruous.

'I've been dreading this!' said Ian to himself.

'Who is it, Dad?'

Dick spotted them and saw the chance for some drama.

'Your father's a bad man, son,' he said in an American accent. 'I've come to take him away and lock him up.'

Ian was pleased but not a little unnerved to see him. They hugged each other in greeting and laughed.

'What are you doing here?' said Ian. 'Where did you get that car? And that suit? You look terrific.'

'I am.' Dick turned to the boy. 'You must be Alan.'

'You must be rich,' said Alan, eyeing the car.

'I've had my moments. My name is Dick Dobson. Your father and I were Rommel's deadliest enemies.'

'Are you the one who talked about fishing in the middle of the desert?'

'That's me – when I wasn't killing Germans.'

Alan marvelled at him. Here was a real soldier at last.

Ian studied the car. 'You've nicked it, haven't you?'

'I have not!' said Dick with righteous indignation. 'I am on an important humanitarian mission. And if you stop being peevish, I'll let you come as well.'

'Only if you let me drive.'

'All yours,' said Dick, handing over the key.

The two of them got into the car and Alan panicked.

'What do I tell Mum?' he asked.

'The truth,' said Ian, revving up.

'She won't believe it.'

The car moved smoothly away and turned the corner. Ian was enjoying himself. He put his foot down on the accelerator and they surged effortlessly forward. Dick let out a yell of alarm and clutched the sides of his seat.

'Relax,' said Ian. 'I'm only doing thirty . . . Hey, why aren't you on the farm?'

'I felt the call of the metropolis.'

'You mean your Dad chucked you out?'

'Nope. I never went home.' He blanched at the car's erratic progress. 'Careful!'

Ian swerved violently. 'You what?' he said, moving to the correct side of the road again. 'Didn't go back?'

'Couldn't face it, Ian. I want excitement, colour, music. Not sheep and pig shit.' Another crash threatened. 'Keep your eyes on the bloody road!'

Ian dodged an ancient Riley. 'Sorry,' he said and drove more carefully. 'So you turned your back on the land, eh?'

'What about you?'

'Everything's fine.'

'Work?'

'Work's work.'

'Wife and kid? He's a nice lad.'

'Great. I couldn't be happier.'

He spoke with conviction but Dick Dobson knew his pal too well to be deceived. He sensed the disillusion.

'You're bored out of your tiny mind, aren't you?'

Ian drove on, his gaze fixed firmly on the road.

Janet Deasey kept going to the window every time she heard footsteps on the pavement but there was never any sign of her husband. She had made a lot of allowances for Ian since his return but even her patience had its limits. She heard a car approaching and she pressed her nose hopefully against the pane of glass, only to see a taxi rattle past. Exasperation made her turn back to Alan, who was reading a comic in one of the armchairs.

'A friend from the Army, was he?' she said.

'Dick, his name was. He's a fisherman, too.'

'With a big American car?'

'Yes, it was fantastic!'

'Did they say where they were going?'

'A human . . . humanitarian mission.'

She was sceptical. 'Down at the pub, probably.'

'Don't be mad at him. Dad's only been home a week.'

'Exactly!'

Her mouth hardened and she went to the window again.

Ian Deasey and Dick Dobson strolled happily into the garage where they had left the car for an hour while they adjourned to the nearest bar. The mechanic who had taken the vehicle from them was now polishing it with a cloth. He gave Dick a broad wink to indicate that the boot had been loaded with the items for delivery. Dick gave him a wave of thanks then got into the car with Ian, making sure that he was behind the driving wheel this time.

Ian was fascinated by something his friend told him.

'What's the name of the club?' he said.

'Les Girls.'

'And what's the name of their act?'

'Tommy and Jerry,' said Dick. 'Only it's *our* act.'

'They pinched our material?'

'Lock, stock and Rommel. Bloody nerve! Let's get our own back on the sods, shall we?'

The car set off and they chuckled with glee. They parked outside the club in Soho and went down the stairs. Ian had already had too much to drink to notice how seedy the place was, and, when a complimentary glass of whisky was placed in his hand, he thought he was in heaven. The floor show had just begun and he was entranced by Hedda as she led the dancing troupe through their routine. Nobody clapped as loud as him at the end. Les Girls was living up to its name.

Scott and Hodges then stepped into the limelight and introduced themselves as Tommy and Jerry. Ian hooted. The terrible twins clicked straight into their stolen act.

'Did I ever tell you of the time I took on a German panzer single-handed?' said Scott.

'Don't think so, old horse,' replied Hodges.

'We were pinned down outside Tobruk. I was separated from the troop. I'd been doing dangerous sabotage work behind enemy lines . . . I came round the corner of a wadi.'

'What's a wadi, then?' prompted Ian.

'Yes, what *is* a wadi?' said Hodges.

'It's like a khazi. Only bigger.'

'So they can get the camels in,' yelled Ian, getting the biggest laugh yet. 'The turret slowly rotated . . . '

'The turret slowly rotated in my direction,' said Scott,

shaken by the interruptions. 'The turret slowly . . . '

'Didn't you have a sink plunger?' said Ian.

'Luckily I had my sink plunger.'

'Just in case,' added Ian.

'Just in case,' repeated Scott.

But their act was already over. Ian's interruptions were much funnier than Tommy and Jerry who made ever more frenzied attempts to control their audience. The erstwhile second lieutenants were completely buried beneath the jeers and the boos. When Ian had thoroughly ruined their act, he went outside to get some fresh air. He wanted to clear his head before going home. He came up into the street in time to see Costas, the club's proprietor, standing beside the open boot of the limousine as burly men unloaded boxes from it. Ian was sobered at once. He pointed an accusing finger.

'Oi!' he shouted. 'What's your game?'

'It's OK,' said Costas. 'We can manage.'

'That's not your bloody car!'

Ian went charging back down the stairs and into the club. Dick was having a drink at the bar and chatting to Hedda. Ian rushed over to him, whispered in his ear and dragged him out. The two of them went hurtling back up the steps and out into the street, where Ian tried to grab a box from one of the men. They fought angrily over it until the box fell to the ground and split open. Dozens of glossy pornographic magazines spilled out. Dick picked one up and studied it with bleary eyes.

'Tits and bums!' he said. 'What the hell's going on?'

'This is all paid for!' snarled Costas. 'What's the matter with you?'

Dick had no time to answer. The night was suddenly full of sound and fury as bells clanged on police cars and bright headlights swept into the streets. It was a raid. Ian was the first to react. Grabbing Dick by the arm, he ran over to the limousine as fast as he could.

'Get in, Dick!' he urged. 'Get in! Quick!'

Police cars were already screeching to a halt outside the club. Dick dived into the vehicle as Ian gunned the motor. In the panic, Ian managed to put the car into reverse. It lurched crazily backwards, felling a pile of cardboard boxes, knocking over two dustbins and scattering an army of howling cats.

'Forwards!' pleaded Dick. 'Forwards!'

Ian found the right gear and the car went forwards with a fierce plunge of speed, bouncing off a lamppost and grazing the wing of yet another police car which had just pulled up. Pandemonium reigned. As he glanced through the window, Dick could see the protesting Costas being arrested by uniformed constables. Someone must have tipped off the police. The raid was well-timed. They had been caught red-handed.

Fear turned Ian into a mad racing driver. Getting full power out of the limousine, he corkscrewed his way through the streets of Soho, narrowly escaping disaster at every turn. He rode his luck on four wheels, and on two, until it finally ran out. Careering wildly along a narrow street, he lost control, and the motor mounted the pavement to demolish a line of market stalls and the barrows that were innocently standing by. The vehicle juddered to a halt.

Ian was disgusted at the thought that his friend might be a spiv and involved in all kinds of shady dealings, but Dick was much more concerned with the state of Lorimer's car. It had taken a terrible battering and smoke was rising from under the bonnet.

'Look what you've done!' wailed Dick.

Ian was outraged. 'What *I've* done!'

CHAPTER 4

The three of them stood beside the inspection ramp in the garage like mourners attending a funeral. The limousine looked even more sorry for itself in the daylight. It had dents and scratches everywhere, and a deep crater in one door. Those were only the visible wounds. With the bonnet up, the mechanic was checking the damage to the engine and itemizing its defects on an oil-stained pad. A beautiful car had been comprehensively wrecked.

Dick Dobson watched in respectful silence with a grim-faced Major Lorimer and a scowling Colonel Palliser at his side. He feared dreadful repercussions from the two men. Dick had been entrusted with a superb limousine and this was the result. He braced himself as the mechanic finished his inspection and reeled off the appalling list of injuries.

'Radiator cracked and leaking. Engine block shifted. Oil sump split. Fan belt snapped.' He walked around the car to point out the exterior defects. 'Front bumper ruined. Bonnet scraped. Off-side panels wrecked. Quarterlight smashed. Door mountings —'

Rudi Lorimer held up a hand to stop him then he turned to Dick Dobson. The latter shivered with apprehension. Instead of giving him a roasting, however, Lorimer emitted a sudden laugh and clapped him on the back.

'What's the matter, Richard!' he said jovially. 'You look like you've seen a ghost.'

Dick blinked. 'You mean, you're not angry?'

'Cars!' Lorimer waved a dismissive hand. 'Two-a-penny! Who cares?' He led Dick out of the garage. 'Forget it.'

'We were set up,' complained Dick.

'You may be right.'

'Someone phoned the police.'

'I wonder who that could have been,' said Palliser as he joined them, sharing a private smile with his colleague. 'You can't trust anybody these days.'

'The main thing is that *you* were not caught, Richard,' said Lorimer. 'Only that greasy little bastard, Costas.'

'I thought he was your business partner,' said Dick.

'Not any more!'

'So where do we go from here?'

'I have a little surprise for you.'

Dick grew suspicious. 'It's not illegal, is it?'

Lorimer looked hurt and insulted by the suggestion. 'Richard!'

Ian Deasey never did things by half-measures. When he had a hangover, it was always in the championship class. He was sitting behind his desk at the council offices that morning, supporting his chin on both hands while the battle of El Alamein was fought out inside his skull. Every turret was rotating quickly in his direction, aiming shells at him with devastating accuracy. His whole body quivered as he suffered another direct him. What use was a sink-plunger now?

He closed his eyes and heard another noise amid the next round of explosions. It was the sound of a waterfall. It got louder and louder. Ian could almost feel the spray dotting his face but, when he lifted his leaden eyelids, he found himself staring at a glass of Alka Seltzer that June had considerately set down in front of him.

'Try that,' said the secretary. 'It'll do you good.'

'I couldn't touch a thing,' groaned Ian.

'Drink it down, Mr Deasey.'

'They kept saying that to me last night.'

'How are you feeling now?'

'Ready to sign my will.'

'If there's anything else you need . . . '

'Thanks, June. You're an angel.'

The secretary bobbed away and Ian stared at the glass. It continued to fizz maliciously back at him. El Alamein suffered its fiercest period of fighting. He gripped his temples to hold the bombardment in. A land-mine went off right beside him. He flinched and saw that a stack of files had been slammed down on his desk by the sadistic Norman.

'Morning, Deasey,' he said with irrepressible glee.

'Ugh!'

'You look terrible, mate.'

'Thank you.'

'Been out on the tiles, have we?' He nudged Ian. 'Bet Mrs Deasey's glad of a rest, eh? Four years on short rations then home you come. I know what you soldiers are!'

'Norman . . . '

'Like rabbits!'

'Norman . . . '

'Take pity on her.'

'Norman,' said Ian, politely.

'Yes?'

'Sod off!'

His colleague went off laughing and Ian was left to muse on the multiple follies of a night in Soho with Dick Dobson. He had drunk too much, fought with a bouncer, run from a police raid, crashed a car and taken about ten years off his life. One thought alone offered a crumb of comfort.

His wife had no idea where he had really been.

Janet Deasey was a caring housewife. Now that she had given up her job at the ATS motor pool, she could spend more time keeping the prefab neat and tidy. The unappealing structure might look like something out of a shanty town but it was as clean as a pin on the inside. Having cleared up in the kitchenette, Janet went through to the main bedroom. She clicked her tongue in irritation when she saw Ian's demob suit lying in a crumpled heap. He had arrived home well after midnight in a dreadful state, passing out the moment his head hit the pillow. She could smell the drink.

Getting him up and ready for work had been a Herculean task but she had somehow managed it, helping him into the sports coat and flannels that she had picked up for him from a local second-hand clothes shop. Between lurching visits to the bathroom, Ian had apologized profusely and told her that he had been out with the boys and lost track of time. He promised that it would not happen again. Janet's anger had softened. It seemed cruel to attack a man who was already writhing in agony. She tried to be broad-minded. Adjusting to civilian life was bound to be difficult and Ian was entitled to go off the rails slightly. His obvious pain was punishment enough for his night out.

Janet took a hanger from the wardrobe and slipped the jacket of the suit on to it. She then picked up the trousers and held them by the turn-ups to straighten them out. Something fell from one of the pockets and landed on the carpet. She bent down to pick up a cocktail stick with a little flag attached to it. The name of a Soho night-club was printed on it in bold type – LES GIRLS.

She twisted the stick between her fingers and pondered. If Ian Deasey had been out with the boys, who were these girls?

Major Rudi Lorimer was a born organizer. Dick Dobson had noticed before that his friend had an uncanny knack of getting things down with maximum efficiency. He was given further proof of the fact when Lorimer and Palliser took him along to Soho that afternoon in a taxi. As the three of them got out, Dick recognized the dismal back street from which he and Ian had fled so ignominiously in the limousine and he shuddered at the memory. He had no wish to see Les Girls night-club ever again.

Rudi Lorimer once again seemed to read his mind.

'You will not see Les Girls,' he promised.

'But it's right in front of me,' said Dick.

'Look more carefully.'

Dick Dobson squinted up at the sign above the door and his jaw dropped. What had once been Les Girls was now called The Blue Parrot. The new sign was bold yet tasteful and much more alluring. Men on ladders were giving the exterior of the place a fresh lick of paint and the rickety staircase had been miraculously replaced.

'Down we go!' said Lorimer, leading the way.

'After you, Dick,' invited the smirking Palliser.

'Oh, right. Thanks.'

The improvements to the outside of the building were nothing compared to the radical alterations that were taking place inside. When they entered the club itself, Dick was astounded. Builders and decorators were swarming all over the place and they had already transformed it from a seedy dive into something much more luxurious.

Dick Dobson whistled in frank admiration.

'Fantastic! It must be costing a bomb.'

'Nothing but the best for me,' said Lorimer smoothly.

'And you *own* the club now?'

'For my sins, Richard.'

'What happened to old Costas?'

'Sad business,' said Palliser. 'They discovered that his papers were forged and that he was living here as an illegal immigrant. Somebody must have tipped the police off about him.'

'Yes,' said Lorimer, stepping behind the bar. 'Probably the same chap who told them when to raid this place. That informer did a public service. I'd like to meet him.' He winked at Palliser then took a bottle of champagne from a waiting ice bucket. 'I'd like to buy the fellow a drink.' The cork popped, the bubbles gushed and Lorimer quickly filled three champagne glasses. He handed the first to Palliser. 'There you are.'

Dick took his glass and Lorimer proposed a toast.

'To our dear deported friend, Constantine Costas!'

'May he rot in Hellas!' said Palliser.

Dick was not at all sure what was going on but one thing was certain. It was vintage champagne of the highest quality. Rudi Lorimer did things in style. The new owner of the club surveyed his empire with cultured pride.

'In the war,' he said airily, 'who do you think shot down the most planes?'

'The RAF,' said Dick loyally.

'Wrong, my friend. It was not the gallant English. It was the Aussies, the South Africans, the Polacks. The ones who didn't play to the rules.' He put a hand on Dick's shoulder. 'Nothing's changed, old boy. So – make up your mind. Do you want to live on rations and margarine, or do you want to spread your butter thick?'

Dick Dobson needed only a second to consider it.

'Well, if you're offering . . . ' he said.

Lorimer smiled. 'I'm offering.'

Her whole wardrobe had vanished in the bombing raid that destroyed their house, and since then Janet Deasey had been forced to make do with an array of second-hand garments. They were all so dowdy and unfashionable. Ian's gift was thus an especially welcome surprise. She tried it on in the bedroom that evening. It was a silk dress, which hugged her body like a doting lover and showed off her figure to best advantage. She loved the feel of the material and stroked it sensuously. She admired herself in the mirror and was thrilled with the result. Janet Deasey was a sexy and attractive woman in her prime. For the first time in years, she believed that she now looked the part.

Her eye fell on the other gifts with which her husband had showered her. The flowers stood in a vase on the dressing table and the box of chocolates – all their sweet coupons for a month! – lay beside it. Ian Deasey had always been a kind and loving husband. He was keen to make amends for the excesses of his night out with Dick Dobson, and Janet had been touched by the efforts to which he had gone on her behalf. But she was still not entirely won over.

The dress was beautiful, the flowers were fragrant and the chocolates were her favourite, but there was another legacy from Ian's night of celebration. She thought of the cocktail stick which had dropped out of his pocket. Where had he been? Why had he spent so much on her? Were all these gifts simply a way of alleviating his guilt? Janet was deeply grateful to him but she would reserve judgement.

An impatient Ian tapped on the bedroom door.

'Give us a look then!' he called.

'Ready!' she said.

The door opened and two heads peeped in. Ian was in shirt and trousers but Alan wore striped pyjamas and a mottled dressing gown. Janet twirled around for their inspection. They were both greatly impressed.

'What d'you think, then?' said Ian.

His son gave a wolf-whistle. 'Not bad, eh, Dad?'

'Alan!' scolded his mother.

The boy ran away laughing and Ian stepped into the bedroom and closed the door after him. Arms wide in sheer wonder, he beamed happily at his wife.

'Not bad at all.'

'You're worse than he is.'

'I've had more practice.' They laughed. 'Hey, have you noticed? He's started to call me "Dad" again.'

'Well, you are his Dad,' she said. 'And my husband.'

She stepped up to him and he caught the aroma of her perfume. Ian slipped his arms around her and felt the delicious softness of the silk. His face was a mask of contrition.

'Am I forgiven?' he said.

'Possibly . . . '

'What else do I have to do?'

'We'll come to that.'

She gave a giggle and rubbed her nose against his. Ian was about to kiss her when there was a banging on the door.

'Hey, Dad!' called Alan.

'Go away!'

'Is your funny friend coming back?'

'No, son. They won't allow him out again.'

'What do you mean?' asked the boy.

'Time for bed, young man,' said Janet.

'Yes,' reinforced Ian. 'Scarper!'

They heard him go into his own bedroom and relaxed. Ian held her close again. The new dress had been an inspiration. A thought now struck her.

'Ian,' she said, 'we should go up West some time.'

'Yes, yes. Why not?'

'Apparently, there's a club in Soho called Les Girls . . .'

He backed away in alarm. 'No, no, Janet,' he said, querulously. 'There wouldn't be any point in going there.'

'Why not?'

'Because it's . . . not a very nice place.'

'You've been?'

'No,' he lied, 'but I know someone who has.'

'Your friend Dick Dobson by any chance?'

'Yes, that's right. Said it's a low, despicable dive.'

'I see.' Her eye twinkled. 'So any decent married man who strayed in there by mistake would find it so disgusting that he'd never visit the place again.'

'Never!' he affirmed. 'Never, never, never!'

'I hoped you'd say that.'

'Forget about Soho night-clubs,' he urged. 'Stick to your Gilbert and Sullivan. Good, wholesome stuff. Anyway, why spend money on entertainment when you can make your own?'

Janet leaned forward to kiss him full on the lips.

'I thought you'd never ask . . . '

Ian Deasey felt in such high spirits next morning that he even gave the egregious Norman a smile as he went into work. Life was good. He had a family, a job, a place in the scheme of things. It was time to count his blessings. Seated at his desk, he reviewed his situation and came to the conclusion that he could be a lot worse off. Within seconds, he was. The unwanted face of Dick Dobson suddenly materialized in the corridor and the nightmare started all over again. Ian dived for cover behind his desk but he had already been spotted.

Dick let himself into the office and walked across.

'What the hell are *you* doing here!' said Ian. 'Go away!'

'That's no way to greet your old pal.'

'Down!'

Ian had seen Frank Parsons coming into the office and did not wish to be caught entertaining a visitor. He yanked Dick down behind the desk and told him to shut up, but his friend, thinking it was some kind of game, pretended that they were under fire in the desert.

'Look out, Ian! There's a big one coming over now!'

It turned out to be Frank Parsons, leaning over the desk with his eyebrows twitching away. Ian got to his feet at once but Dick started to inspect the carpet as if searching for something. His hand fell on a tiny object.

'Ah, there's another one,' he said. 'Pesky little blighters, paper clips.'

'Who is this person?' enquired the Borough Surveyor.

'Captain Dobson,' said Dick, levering himself up with difficulty as if feeling the effects of an old war wound. 'Dick Dobson, Royal Engineers.' He pumped Parsons's hand. 'It's taken me such a long time to find him, Mister – '

'Parsons.'

'Mister Parsons. This man saved my life.'

'Did he?' Parsons was amazed by the news.

'Yes. If it wasn't for Ian Deasey, I wouldn't be here today.' That bit at least was, technically, true. 'I had to come. You understand.'

'Ian.' His boss turned to him. 'You never said anything.'

'He wouldn't,' Dick assured him.

'No,' agreed Ian.

'You can deal with this any time, Ian,' said Parsons expansively. 'You and your friend will want to have a quiet moment together, won't you? Go on. Go across the road for an hour. You can make it up at the end of the day.' He smiled at Dick. 'I'm glad to have met you, Mister – '

'Dobson. Captain Dobson.'

Parsons shook his hand again then departed at speed.

'I'll bloody kill you!' warned Ian.

A few minutes later, they were going into the pub across the road and Ian was warming to his theme. He did not notice the old lady who sat at a table, nursing a glass of stout. She heard every word of his tirade.

'Why don't you go back to your farm and leave me alone?' demanded Ian. 'First, you try to get me killed being chased around Soho by the police, then you nearly lose me my job with some story about me saving your life! Well, I wouldn't save your life, not in a million years!'

'Not very nice, Deasey,' observed Dick. 'Not very Christian. Especially as I'm the one who saved your life.'

'You did not.'

'I did, too.' The barman approached. 'A pint for me, please, my good fellow. And a half for my friend here.'

'I don't want a drink!' howled Ian.

'Nerves, you know,' explained Dick, leaning over to the old lady whose mouth was now agape. He turned back to Ian. 'Don't you remember Sicily? When we had to do that bridge?'

'No.'

'When we got shot up by that American plane.'

'No.'

'Well, we did. And I saved your life.'

'You did not.'

'I did so.' The barman had pulled the pint and Dick took a quick sip from it. 'At great risk to myself and regardless of enemy fire, I saved your bacon.'

'How?'

'I warned you.'

'It was a plane!' said Ian. 'I heard it coming.'

'Only because I alerted you in the nick of time.'

'You dived in a trench and shouted "Help, help! Those bastards are trying to kill me!"'

'Exactly.' Dick grinned at him. 'I warned you.'

Ian grabbed the pint tankard and drank deeply from it.

'What do you want?' he said warily. 'If it's another dirty book delivery, you can forget it.'

'I have a little proposition for you . . . '

'No,' said Ian firmly. 'Whatever it is!'

☆ ☆ ☆

The Blue Parrot Club was open for business and packed with a much more select clientele. Gone were the drunken squaddies and the lonely men in long macs. Gentlemen in dinner jackets or in officers' uniform now lounged at the tables, attended by sexily clad hostesses and paying high prices for fine wines. Hedda was now the leading hostess and she glided around the club in the slinkiest dress this side of decency. She threw a smile towards the stage where the performers were having a wonderful time, even if most of the audience were too inebriated or preoccupied to listen to them.

Ian Deasey was wearing an ill-fitting dinner jacket while Dick Dobson, in more elegant attire, sat at the piano and accompanied his partner. They sang in pleasing harmony.

'On Soho streets, everyone one meets is gay.
And all the ladies are inclined to ask one in to pass the time.
Though it has to be said, some stay in bed all day,
Because they have to earn a living.
And they do it giving pleasure – and it pays!'

The longer they went on, the more Ian enjoyed it all. It was a delight to perform in such an intimate space with such a captivating atmosphere. He brought their act to a close with a highly amended version of 'Lily of Laguna'.

'She is my Fanny Fox from Fulham.
She's got a fanny . . . and she . . . '

There was a ragged cheer and the two artistes took their bow before vacating the stage for the dancing girls. Dick led Ian across to the bar. Double gins were waiting for them.

'Well done, Deasey. I think we managed to lower the tone.'

'I'm appalled that such filth should be allowed in a public place,' said Ian with mock indignation. 'I intend to complain to the proprietor.'

'Go ahead,' said Dick, 'for I am he.'

'Who?'

'You have the honour to address the manager of the Blue

Parrot Club. Richard Dobson, gent.'

Ian was startled. 'Who's idea was that, then?'

'The excellent Major Lorimer's.'

'The crook who set you up with the dirty books?'

'A simple mistake, complicated by your involvement.'

'I see,' said Ian, doubtfully.

Dick gazed around. 'So how would you feel about making this a regular fixture?' he said.

'What – doing "Fanny Fox"?'

'A sophisticated cabaret act, yes.'

Ian was tempted. 'For *money*?'

'Subject to negotiation with the management.'

Janet Deasey was fast asleep in the armchair with the light still on. Wearing her silk dressing gown, she had been ready for bed for hours but had wanted to wait until her husband returned. A toilet flushed romantically nearby then a bleary-eyed Alan shuffled in and shook her gently.

'Ian?' she said,waking. 'Oh, it's you, Alan . . . '

'I couldn't sleep.'

'What time is it?'

'Well past midnight. D'you think Dad's all right?'

'For the time being,' she said grimly. 'Come on. Bed.'

She led her son out and switched off the light.

The dancing troupe had also been a revelation. They were the same girls but their act was at once more artistic and more daring. When the troupe left the stage, the band played a smokey waltz and the hostesses encouraged the customers to get up and dance with them. Several couples were soon smooching dreamily to the music.

Ian Deasey was about to leave when Hedda came up.

'I trust that you've been paid,' she said.

'Mister Deasey is a gentleman amateur,' said Dick.

'He must have some reward for his act,' she argued. 'Would the gentleman amateur like to dance?'

Ian was flabbergasted. 'You're asking me?'

'Who else?' she purred.

'I'm married.'

'I want to dance with you, not have your children.'

Ian began to make his excuses but his voice tailed off. He

had just had a marvellous evening and the most beautiful woman in the room was offering to dance with him. He grinned vacuously and let her lead him on to the floor. Major Lorimer sidled up to Dick and the pair of them looked on with satisfaction. Everyone was having a wonderful time.

Mellow music played over the swaying dancers. Hedda was wrapped around Ian, pulling him to the rippling contours of her body and brushing his cheek with her lips. He was overwhelmed. Ian Deasey was in Elysium.

Walthamstow was a million miles away.

CHAPTER 5

Another night brought another batch of eager patrons in to sample the delights of the Blue Parrot Club, allowing Dick Dobson and Ian Deasey to perform before an appreciative audience. Their act now had a professional sheen and they had even found a dinner jacket which looked marginally less ridiculous on Ian. Basking in the spotlight, they reached the climax of their turn, singing in unison as Dick banged out the tune of 'The Man Who Broke the Bank at Monte Carlo':

'As I stroll along St Martin's Lane,
With a swagger in my stride,
You can hear the girls confide,
"He must have some put aside".
And I don't deny, I've a bit put by,
For a rainy day, so I walk this way,
I'm the wag who doped the nag
That lost the Derby!

And I saunter down to Soho Square,
With a self-supported air,
And I'm greeted everywhere,
For the tarts all know me there.
And I might decide to take a ride,
If it's free of germs and the going's firm,
I'm the wag who . . . '

The audience joined in the last two lines then clapped and cheered. Dick joined his partner at the centre of the stage to take a bow and milk the applause, then he announced the next act with a flourish.

'Gentlemen!' he said. 'Your attention, please, for the

Blue Parrot's feathered friends!'

The band went into an up-tempo samba and Hedda led on the troupe. They were all costumed in feathers as birds of paradise and it was clearly the moulting season. Whoops of delight went up as more and more bare flesh was revealed. Hedda performed the most mesmerizing fan-dance of all. The Blue Parrot was getting bluer by the minute.

Alone in the gents' cloakroom, Ian Deasey was half out of his dinner jacket and half into his motorbike gear when a young subaltern came wandering in. He wore a black tie and was clearly a junior officer having a night out. He swayed alcoholically.

'Is this the gents?' he asked.

'I hope so,' said Ian.

'It's you!' He shook Ian's hand with enthusiasm. 'You were awfully good. Capital!'

'Thank you.'

'Very clever stuff, old chap.'

'I'm glad you enjoyed it.'

'Oh, I did. First class. Name's Elwood . . . '

The effort of recalling his own name seem to drain all his strength and he almost collapsed against a wall but he righted himself to blurt out a slurred invitation.

'Charge of organizing this thing. Officers' bash. Needs an act with a bit of – fizz! You two would be ideal.'

'Thanks,' said Ian tolerantly. 'If you remember anything in the morning, bear us in mind.'

Elwood rolled off harmlessly into a cubicle and struck up a conversation with the cistern. Ian smiled and changed quickly into his gear. His motorbike was in the alley at the side of the club and he was soon weaving his way home through the stillness of the night. When he finally reached Walthamstow, he switched off his engine at the end of his road and let the machine coast along to his prefab. He parked the motorbike as quietly as he could. Fatigue made him lurch unsteadily towards the door.

He let himself in and went straight to the bedroom, but his attempts to tiptoe backfired. Ian fell against the wardrobe with an almighty thud and brought Janet instantly awake. She sat up to see a sinister, masked intruder.

'Oh, my God!' she gasped.

'It's me, love.'

'Ian! Take that bloody helmet off.'

'Sorry.'

She yawned. 'What time is it?'

'Around midnight,' he said, quickly undressing.

Janet put on the bedside lamp to peer at the alarm clock. 'It's a quarter past two!' she complained.

'Got paid tonight. Ten quid. It's in the sugar tin.'

'It'll cover your medical expenses when you come off that bike from exhaustion on your way home.'

'Don't be daft.' He put on his pyjamas. 'And I got complimented by a very senior officer tonight.'

'Deaf, was he?'

'No. Blind drunk.' He got into bed beside her.

'You're freezing!' she hissed. 'Hey, did you remember it's Alan's birthday on Friday?'

'Of course.' He paused. 'Who's Alan?'

'Your son and heir to the Deasey sugar tin.' She switched off the light and snuggled up to him. 'Well, as you're here, you might as well make yourself useful.' She waited for action. 'Ian.' No answer. 'Ian!'

A first snore sounded. He was dead to the world.

Dick Dobson was alone in the empty club, smoking a cigarette and playing a melody on the piano. Hedda drifted in with a coat around her shoulders and sang a few bars of the song. Even intoxicated, Dick recognized the quality of her voice.

'Always wanted to accompany a woman,' he confessed. 'Gracie, Vera Lynn. Their hard luck . . . Where d'you learn?'

'I picked it up from my father, I suppose. He was a crooner.' She helped him up from the piano. 'Come on.'

'Where's your dad now?' he asked.

'In heaven, I hope. Waiting for Bing Crosby to come and sing duets of 'White Christmas' with him.' She steered Dick towards the exit. 'Dad never had much luck. He moved to the country to escape the blitz and a Lancaster Bomber on a training flight crash-landed on his cottage.'

'I'm sorry.'

'He would have seen the funny side.'

They sauntered out and locked the door after them.

What happened then, Dick did not really know. All that he could recall was being taken to an ear-splitting jazz club nearby, feeling a sense of vague danger and drinking treble whiskies. The next minute – or so it seemed – someone slapped him on the rump and he came awake in a strange room. He struggled to open an eye and to take his bearings.

'Where am I?' he groaned.

'You got into my bed,' said Hedda from the bathroom.

'Oh, no. I'm sorry . . . and?'

'And you were a perfect gentleman.'

'Was I?'

'You took off your shoes and you didn't throw up. What more could a girl ask?'

Dick rolled over and saw that he was in a large bed-sitter with furnishings that had a transatlantic feel. There were even a few American pennants on the wall. He was lying half-dressed on a bed that was draped in lace. He saw the photograph on the table and squinted at the smiling face of an American airman. Hedda appeared in the doorway. Her long fair hair was whisked up into bangs.

'Old boyfriend?' he said, gazing at the photo.

'Old husband. Eddie.'

'Oh, God!' Fearing complications, he heaved himself off the bed. 'Where is he? Eddie, that is.'

'I don't know.' She gave a shrug. 'Missing in action.'

'Oh dear!' He saw the clock. 'It's half past nine!'

'Relax. Plenty of time before we need to leave.' She crossed the room. 'I'll be back in an hour. Sweet dreams.'

Hedda went out and Dick sat on the edge of the bed.

How on earth did he get there?

When Ian Deasey arrived at his desk, the mounds of paperwork on it were significantly higher than anywhere else in the office. Everyone toiled dutifully away as he flopped into his chair and sat back with a yawn. Frank Parsons and the odious Norman descended on him like a pair of vultures.

Ian managed a lop-sided smile of welcome.

'Morning, Mr Parsons,' he said. 'Morning, Norman.'

'It *isn't* morning, Deasey,' snapped his boss, looking at the famous pocket watch. 'It's seven minutes past twelve. Norman and his lads have been sitting idle for hours.'

'That's not very good, Norman,' chided Ian.

'Waiting for *your* instructions!' said Parsons.

'My instructions? Oh yes, yes. Of course.'

Ian remembered that he was meant to give Norman the address of the next house that was due for demolition so that the squad could move into action. In the hope of inspiration, Ian turned to the calendar on the wall and looked for the right date.

'That is the wrong month!' corrected Parsons.

'Is it? Oh, yes. So it is.'

Norman laughed. 'Good old Deasey. Never misses a trick. It's a giggle a minute when he's around.'

Ian did his best to look businesslike and instituted a thorough search of his files. Parsons waited impatiently and Norman grinned mockingly. After scattering excuses at his boss, Ian finally located the relevant details. He read them out as if announcing a train departure at Paddington.

'Here we go,' he boomed. 'Alder Street. Number 23. Bomb damage to roof and cellar walls. It's all yours, Norman. Off you go. Can't have you sitting around here all morning!'

Norman chuckled and went out. Parsons stared at Ian with patent anxiety and then walked off, shaking his head.

Old Glory fluttered over the entrance of the United States Embassy. Marine sentries were on guard at the door as Hedda passed through into the waiting area. Notice-boards were covered with lists and with regulations. She knew exactly where to look and ran her finger down an interminable column of names.

A young, black GI in uniform came across to her.

'Hi again, Mrs Kennedy,' he said with a smile.

'Hello, Oliver.'

'Any luck?'

'Luck?' She indicated the list. 'These are the dead. I don't exactly want to find my husband here.'

'Sure,' he said sympathetically. 'Sorry. But we get new names in all the time. Guys who pulled through. You never know.'

'Anything you hear. *Please.* Anything.'

'Yeah,' he promised. 'Anything.'

Hedda Kennedy thanked him. Oliver was a real friend.

☆ ☆ ☆

Concealed behind the files on his desk, Ian Deasey flicked through the pages of a magazine. Something caught his eye and he drew a circle around it with his fountain pen. He was about to mark another item when he heard the tell-tale tread of Frank Parsons. The magazine was stuffed swiftly under a file and Ian began to write on a sheet of paper, copying the document beside him with easy fluency. When Parsons loomed above him, Ian looked up with a grin, his hand continuing to flow across the page in order to impress his boss.

'Good afternoon, Mr Parsons,' he said.

The Borough Surveyor was sardonic. 'It works better with ink,' he said.

Ian glanced down and saw that the fountain pen had dried up. The last three lines he had written were mere scratches on the page. He stared accusingly at the pen as if a major betrayal had taken place, then looked guiltily up at Parsons. The Borough Surveyor's face was a tombstone of regret.

Dick Dobson and Hedda Kennedy reached Dover as the boat was docking and they waited at the Arrivals barrier to watch the passengers disembark. There was no sign of the people whom they had come to meet and they turned to a Customs Officer. He was a short, serious man in uniform.

'Can you help us, please?' said Dick. 'We're waiting for three French ladies who sailed on the Rothsay.'

'Friends of yours, are they?'

'More sort of colleagues.'

'You'd better come with me.'

Dick and Hedda ducked under the barrier and followed him into a bare, featureless office. He told them to wait a minute and then disappeared for the best part of two hours. Dick and Hedda kicked their heels with increasing irritation. The man finally returned with a senior colleague in tow, a tall, brisk, no-nonsense individual. It was the latter who now took charge.

'You were enquiring about three French women?' he said.

'Yes,' said Dick, wearily. 'Ages ago.'

'We have detained them.'

'But why? What for?'

'For smuggling, sir. For carrying perfume, liquor, tobacco and two suitcases of nylons.'

Dick snorted. 'That's ridiculous!'

'No, sir,' said the senior officer, pedantically. 'That's contraband.' His eyes narrowed with suspicion. 'What exactly is your connection with these three ladies, sir?'

Dick hesitated, shot a glance at Hedda, then invested as much authority in his voice as he could. It was time to put these officious customs men in their place.

'I am proud to call them colleagues,' he said firmly. 'The three ladies whom you are "detaining" are former members of the French Resistance. I am to escort them to a ceremony at the Guildhall, where they are to be presented with the George Cross. If they fail to appear, questions will be asked in high places.'

'Yes, sir. And I'm asking them.'

'Are you seriously telling me that they are in custody over a bottle of scent!' Dick was scandalized. 'These ladies are national heroines!'

'Funny they never mentioned it,' said the other, drily.

'Are they likely to?' Dick was blustering. 'They spent the war avoiding Fascists in uniform like you!'

The man smiled and put on an I-wasn't-born-yesterday expression. To Dick's consternation, even Hedda was laughing at him. She decided to use a different brand of charm on the senior Customs Officer. She took him aside so that she could speak in confidence to him. Batting her eyelids, she gave him a broad smile that made him go weak at the knees.

'Take no notice of my friend's imagination,' she said.

'Very fertile, madam.'

'Madam!' she complained. 'Do I look that old?'

'No, no. Of course not. Quite the contrary.'

'Call me Hedda.'

'Thank you . . . er, Hedda.'

She stepped in close. 'May I confide in you, officer?'

'I hope you will.'

'The young ladies are actresses, over here for a show at the Prince of Wales. And my producer is going to kill me if I don't get them to London in time.'

'Kill you?' He swallowed hard. 'Literally?'

'Worse. He'll sack me.'

'Who's egg-head, then?' asked the man, indicating Dick and showing that he understood these things. 'Producer's son?'

'Nephew. Can you help me, officer? Please.'

Her eyes were pools of delight and he wallowed in them for a full minute before wading to the bank. He took her over to Dick.

'Tell your uncle that he's very lucky indeed to have this young lady working for him.'

'My . . . ?' Dick caught on at once. 'Yes, yes. Very lucky. Very lucky, indeed. Does that mean that they'll be released?'

'Without delay.'

'Thank you so much,' murmured Hedda, stroking his arm and giving him the eye treatment once more. 'I'll make sure you get tickets for the show.'

Norman's features were usually aglow with self-esteem but his face was puce with anger as he stormed into the office and made a bee-line for Ian Deasey. The latter was highly amused.

'You look hot, Norman,' he said.

'I am!'

'And bothered.'

'Thanks to you.'

'Man in your position, getting hot and bothered,' said Ian with disapproval. 'Not the kind of thing we expect from a future Deputy Borough Surveyor, you know.'

'They almost lynched me!

'Who did?'

'The people living at 23 Alder Street.'

'What are you on about?'

'The house I was supposed to demolish,' wailed Norman. 'They were sitting there, eating their dinner, when me and my lads came drilling through the kitchen wall.'

'That wasn't very considerate of you, Norman.' Ian went off into a peal of maniacal laughter. 'Bet they were surprised!'

'It was all your fault you idiot!'

'Was it?'

'You sent me to the wrong bloody address.'

'Did I?' His laughter turned to concern. '*Did* I?'

The car drew up opposite the civic buildings and Dick Dobson jumped out of the driver's seat. There was no time to waste.

'Come on!' he shouted.

While Dick ran across the road, Hedda emerged from the car with three stunningly attractive young women in chic dresses and heavy make-up. Hedda cut through their excited chatter with an urgent command.

'*Allez, allez, mes petites!*'

They tottered across the road in their high heels. Dick had now reached the two elderly gentlemen, who were waiting outside the door in morning suits, smoking Woodbines.

'Where's the other one?' said Dick.

'He's gone,' said the first man.

'Gone where?'

'Bowls match. He couldn't wait.'

'You're two hours late,' said the other man. 'It's just me and Ted. I'm Roger, by the way.'

Hedda arrived with the girls and the men shook off their air of boredom at once. They grinned lecherously and began to size up the newcomers.

'What's the problem?' asked Hedda.

'We're a man short,' said Dick.

'I can manage two!' said Ted, ogling the girls.

'Be quiet. Let's get sorted out. Now, who's who?'

'I'm Miss Lacroix,' said Roger.

'Chantal?' called Dick.

'Oui?' said one of the girls.

'You're with this gentleman.'

Chantal turned a contemptuous Gallic stare on Roger, who responded with a hopeful leer. She began to protest loudly to her colleagues. Ted straightened his tie and moved in.

'I'm Madamoiselle Renault,' he said.

'Claudette,' said Hedda.

'*You*?' said another of the girls, looking with disgust at Ted's dirty-old-man smile. 'You are for me?'

'If you say so, love,' he answered then nudged Dick. 'Look, mate, if there's a spare bird going . . . '

Dick ignored him and scanned the road anxiously.

'Where the hell is Henshaw!' he snarled.

'It was the regional finals,' said Roger.

'What are we going to do?' said Hedda, checking her watch. 'They'll be closing soon. We can't stay here.'

'We won't,' said Dick. 'Come on. In we go.'

☆ ☆ ☆

When Ian Deasey went into his boss's office, Frank Parsons was glancing through the copy of *The Stage*, which he had retrieved from Ian's desk. It was the magazine in which his clerk had circled items of interest with his fountain pen. Ian's face fell. He cleared his throat and found a voice.

'Norman says you wanted to see me, Mr Parsons.'

'Yes, Deasey.'

'Norman seems to be in a bad mood.'

'You should meet the family who live in 23 Alder Street,' said Parsons darkly. 'Bad mood? They're livid! They've just been in here demanding they get their fence back.'

Ian stifled a grin. 'Did Norman and his lads . . . ?'

'Flattened it completely.'

Frank Parsons put down *The Stage* and regarded Ian with a mixture of pity and disappointment. His mind ran through his employee's crime sheet and he gritted his false teeth.

'Are you happy in your work, Ian?'

'Deliriously.'

'Be honest. Your heart is not in this job, is it?'

'It is, Mr Parsons!'

'No, I don't think so. We're supposed to be building houses, remember, not knocking them down around the people who live in them.'

'That was a clerical error.'

'One of dozens, Ian. You're just not with us.' He looked down at *The Stage* and read out some of the items that Ian had marked for attention. '"Variety act required, Brighton. Comedian required, Bolton. Singer wanted, Perth . . . " Much more exciting that bomb damage in Walthamstow, don't you think?'

'I don't know.'

'Well, I'm afraid you're going to have to find out,' said Parsons, pronouncing sentence. 'I'm sorry, Ian. Good luck.'

The register office was a large, cold, impersonal room with rows of upright chairs facing a desk. Anything less romantic could not be imagined, and the fussy registrar added to the bleak misery of the occasion. The two elderly bridegrooms did not seem to mind at all. Roger stood beside Chantal with a proprietary smirk while Ted looped his arm through that of Claudette. Both men were clearly interested in the nuptials that were to come rather than the ceremony they had just undergone. The French girls fumed in silence.

Hedda Kennedy waited in the background with a gaggle of witnesses whom she had grabbed on the way in. It was the strangest triple wedding that any of them had ever seen and they looked on with ghoulish fascination as the registrar moved on to the last part of the entertainment.

'And finally,' he droned, 'I call upon these persons here to witness that I . . . ' He consulted a piece of paper on his desk. ' . . . I, Richard Dobson . . . '

'I, Richard Dobson,' repeated Dick with deadpan face.

' . . . do take thee, Marie Lilaque . . . '

'Lalique!' corrected Marie with pert insistence.

'I beg your pardon,' said the registrar. 'Lalique.'

' . . . do take thee, Marie Lalique . . . ' said Dick.

' . . . to be my lawful wedded wife . . . '

Dick contemplated the dreadful step he was taking and squirmed in discomfort. Marie, by contrast, was delighted with her prospective husband. He was far and away the pick of the bunch, and she squeezed his arm affectionately. The other two brides looked on enviously. The registrar prompted Dick with a glance of stern rebuke and the latter capitulated.

' . . . to be my lawful wedded wife . . . ' he muttered.

The registrar went swiftly through the rest of the ceremony then drew himself up to his full height. In all his years of solemnizing holy matrimony, he had never been called upon to preside at such a bizarre event.

'Richard Dobson and Marie Lalique, you have both made the declarations prescribed by law, and have made a solemn and binding contract with each other in the presence of the witnesses here assembled. You are now man and wife together.' Marie giggled but Dick sagged visibly. The registrar addressed all three happy couples. 'You may now – all of you – kiss the brides.'

Ted tried to embrace Claudette but got a ferocious slap across the face. Roger was kept at bay by a warning growl from the lovely Chantal. Dick Dobson alone was accorded the rights due to him at that crucial moment in his life. Marie flung herself at him and planted a production number of a kiss on his unwilling lips. Dick shuddered with terror.

He was married.

CHAPTER 6

Dressed to go to a job that no longer existed, Ian Deasey sat at the table in the kitchenette and pretended to read the *Daily Mirror*. He had not yet found the moment to tell his wife that he had been sacked. Janet was ironing a new dress and humming snatches from Gilbert and Sullivan. He turned a page over.

'Did you know that, if you melted down the entire Royal Navy, you'd have enough metal to build every person in England four prefabs?'

'Is that in the paper?' she said.

'No, I just made it up.'

Janet took the new dress off the ironing board and held it up against her. She was pleased with the result.

'Won't you be late for work, Ian?'

'I was thinking about that . . . ' He began to skirt the dreaded subject warily. 'Maybe I should devote more of my time to, you know, entertaining.'

'Don't be silly!' she said with a laugh. 'Just because you've amused a few drunks in a Soho club . . . '

'Oh.' He was completely deflated. 'Right, well, I'd better get off to work, then.'

He rose to his feet and moved to the door. Janet intercepted him to give him a hug and a kiss. Ian pulled back and tried to summon up enough courage to tell her the awful truth.

'Janet . . . '

'What?'

A lengthy pause. 'Nothing,' he said. 'See you tonight.'

Feeling like an abject coward, he sneaked out.

The address was in central London and he quailed at the sight of such august premises. When he went inside, Ian Deasey felt no less intimidated. Reception was a small but well-appointed room with a smart, efficient-looking young woman at the desk. A nameplate told him that her name was Clare, and she was in the act of answering the telephone. Her tone was clipped and businesslike.

'Marshall Gould's Office . . . I'm sorry, Mr Gould is in a meeting at the moment. If you'd care to call back . . . Thank you.' She replaced the receiver and looked up. 'Yes?'

'I have an appointment,' he said. 'Ian Deasey.'

'Please take a seat, Mr Deasey.'

Ian did so, perching nervously on the edge of an armchair and staring in wonder at the framed photographs of actors and variety artistes on the wall. Marshall Gould was an agent who represented some very illustrious clients.

The phone rang and Clare gave the identical message. She repeated it a third time when a third caller rang. Ian got the impression that Marshall Gould was fiendishly busy in an important meeting. At that moment, a lavatory flushed and the agent himself emerged. His morning conference with *The Times* crossword had been most satisfactory. He tossed the paper down in front of his receptionist.

'Fifteen minutes, eleven seconds. Is that a record?'

'Mr Deasey is here to see you.'

Marshall Gould was a stout man of middle height with the florid face of a heavy drinker and a voice as deep and dark as a disused coalmine. The flamboyant attire made him look younger than his sixty years. He turned a baleful gaze on Ian Deasey and summed him up instantly.

'Comedian.'

'Yes.' Ian laughed nervously. 'Very good.'

'Come in, Mr Deasey . . . '

Marshall Gould led the way into his eyrie. It was even more luxurious than the outer office, and its walls were hidden beneath serried ranks of photographs from grateful clients and a collection of framed playbills. Amid so much talent, Ian felt painfully anonymous. Gould sat behind his huge desk and waved Ian to the chair opposite him. He scrutinized the would-be comedian with a professional cynicism.

'Can you make *me* laugh, Mr Deasey?' he challenged.

'What? Now? Here? No. I mean, well, no.'

'When you feel like being funny,' probed the agent, 'what is it that you feel is funny?'

'The usual, I suppose. Songs and stuff.'

'Any particular venues?'

'Every Naafi from here to Cairo.'

'Too many ENSA rejects about. Any recent experience?'

'The Blue Parrot.'

'Ah.' Gould sighed. ' You sing smutty songs. Before the girls take their clothes off.'

'I want to do better than that,' said Ian bravely.

'A laudable ambition. Are we in a chicken-and-egg situation here?'

'Are we?'

Marshall Gould reclined in his chair, letting the sunlight reflect off his watch-face so that he could direct the beam all over the room and chase it with his eye. He spoke with a patronizing honesty.

'Let me explain, Ian,' he drawled. 'Comedy acts are like wines. Some are best when they're young and fruity. Others need time to mature. Some travel well, and some are only ever good in the region where they're produced. Do you follow me?'

'Not really.'

'Your act. See if it travels. See if it matures. See how you feel in a year or so.'

'A year?' Ian was dejected.

'Are you married?'

'Yes. Why?'

'It's a big step,' warned the agent, aiming the spot of light at the ceiling. 'You need to be sure. *I* need to be sure. Sure that the stage is something that you really want to be on, as opposed to something you're going through.'

The beam of light hit Ian. He blinked in dismay.

Dick Dobson sat at the piano in the Blue Parrot club and toyed idly with the keys. His manner was more languid than ever and he held a long cigarette holder between his teeth. It was several hours before the place opened but it had become his second home, especially since the steward at the Allied Officers' Club started to hound him for payment of his bill. Dick was about to play 'London Pride' when he saw a familar figure coming towards him through the tables.

'Deasey!' he said in suprise. 'Why aren't you at work?'

'I wanted to see what my partner was up to,' said Ian. 'What's that in your mouth?'

'A cigarette holder.'

'What's wrong with your fingers?'

'They're resting.' He played a note on the piano but the key was stiff. He tried it again. 'Why aren't you at that damn silly office, anyway?'

'I've been trying to get *us* work, Dick.'

'Why?' He hammered the key. 'We've got work. Here.'

'Better work,' argued Ian. 'I was speaking to someone. He said we should get our act to travel. Like wine.'

'To travel – like wine?' Dick lifted the piano lid and started to twang the strings inside. 'Who was this genius?'

'An agent. A big agent. We want to get somewhere, don't we?'

'We *are* somewhere, Ian. At the Blue Parrot.'

'I don't think that this is anywhere,' said Ian, annoyed at his partner's lack of interest. 'In fact, it's worse than nowhere.' Dick twanged another string. 'And will you leave that thing alone!

Ian closed the piano lid and almost caught's Dick's fingers. The latter fiddled with his cigarette holder.

'Rudi has great ideas for this place. Expansion.'

'Bigger bums, larger tits.'

'This club is going places.'

At that moment, the three French girls emerged from a door at the rear and spotted Hedda at the bar. They ran across to her, chattering volubly in their native tongue. Ian decided that their work involved rather more than just dancing. Marie saw Dick and paused to blow him a loving kiss. Ian was puzzled.

'She seems to know you.'

'Yes,' said Dick, grimly. 'She's my wife.'

Ian gaped at him in disbelief. Dick was still wondering how to get rid of Marie when he remembered a more immediate problem. The solution might be standing right next to him.

'Listen, Deasey. I'm in a bit of a fix.'

'How many times have I heard that?'

'Would you do me a great favour?'

The steward at the Allied Officers' Club was taken aback when Dick Dobson actually walked up to him and volunteered to settle his account. Ian had come along in support but Dick had forgotten to mention that he was posing as a member of the Royal New Zealand Air Force. The accent startled Ian.

'Let me introduce my batman,' said Dick airily. 'This is Corporal Deasey.'

'Hello.' Ian's New Zealand accent was pure Walthamstow.

'Pop upstairs, Deasey,' ordered Dick. 'Get my kit together. Pronto. Second floor, third on the left.' He beamed at the steward. 'Now, then, John. Where's this bill of mine?'

Ian had been well-primed. Running upstairs to Dick's room, he gathered up as much of his luggage as he could carry and took it down the fire escape before loading it into the sidecar of his waiting motorbike. Dick Dobson's ruse was working. While he himself diverted the steward, Ian cleared out the room for a flit.

It was on the second descent that Ian came unstuck. Dick's golf clubs slid out of their back and clattered down the iron steps before landing on the pavement. Ian went to retrieve them and stuff them haphazardly into the sidecar. A window was thrown up and a voice challenged him.

'What's going on down there!'

Ian looked up in alarm and recognized Elwood. It was the man he had met in the gents' cloakroom the night before.

'Remember me?' he said.

'Of course! Bum tittie. The Blue Whatsit.' He saw a frantic Dick appear further up the fire escape. 'Well, I never. The band's here as well.'

'I'm helping Squadron-Leader Dobson move his personal effects,' explained Ian.

'Faithful batman, eh?'

'We're in a bit of a rush!' said Dick, joining Ian on the pavement and loading up his luggage as fast as he could. 'Get a move on, Deasey.'

But Ian scented an engagement and chatted happily on.

'What happened with that officers' bash?' he said.

'Got the pipes and drums along. Bit of a bore.'

'We might consider an appearance . . . '

'Consider our disappearance!' hissed Dick.

'Gosh!' said Elwood. 'Would you?'

'At a price.'

'What about – I don't know – ten pounds?'

'Each,' insisted Ian.

'That's twenty pounds. Oh dear. Well, why not?' He and Ian shook hands on it. 'Tonight at Chelsea barracks. Twenty one hundred. Cheerio.'

Ian waved to him before he was grabbed from behind by Dick and thrown across the motorbike. An irate steward now came bounding down the fire escape, having discovered the ruse. Dick sat nonchalantly on the pillion as Ian started the motorbike and roared away from the steward's despairing lunge.

They drove to an apartment block in which Dick had a tiny room next to Hedda's. As they brought in the luggage, Ian's face wrinkled in disgust. Dick made light of the cramped conditions and the smell of damp.

'I'm on to a good thing here,' he said.

'Lorimer's using you like a mug,' warned Ian.

'Rudi? He's my friend.'

'Why did you have to marry that girl?'

'It was on impulse. Cupid's arrow.'

'Rubbish! Why isn't she here with you, then?'

'She's at work.'

'Yes,' sneered Ian. 'Giving French lessons. In a little flat above a club in Soho? You've married a tart.'

'We all have to make a living,' said Dick, defensively. 'Why are you so uppity? You've got a steady job, with a pension, and four nights a week in the club for beer money.'

'I don't have a job,' admitted Ian. 'Got the sack.'

'Ah, that explains everything.'

'Look,' said Ian. 'Will you do this concert tonight? You owe me one.' Dick began to protest but Ian had the clinching argument. 'It's twenty quid!'

Cooper's Corsetry was a little shop off the Walthamstow High Street and Edith ran the business with skill and energy. She was stacking the liberty bodices away when the door opened, ringing the little bell. Janet Deasey came barging in with a shopping bag in each hand. She nodded to her mother.

'What brings you here?' said Edith.

'A bit of scrag end.'

'What's he been up to now?'

'I don't mean Alan.'

'Neither do I.'

Edith had never approved of Ian as a son-in-law. Janet went into the cosy living quarters at the rear of the shop and put down her bags on the table. Her mother joined her and took the packet of meat from her. Janet noticed that the table was laid for two people.

'Expecting company, Mum?'

'What? . . . No, no.'

'Why the two places, then?'

'I still forget sometimes, Janet. Your father.'

'Oh, Mum . . . '

She put a consoling arm around her mother but a tender moment was interrupted by the telephone. Edith broke off at once to answer it, using her sing-song professional voice.

'Cooper's Corsetry . . . Who? One moment, please. He's not here but Mrs Deasey is.' She offered the receiver to Janet. 'It's for Ian. Sounds important . . . '

The opportunity to earn ten pounds in Chelsea was vastly more appealing than the prospect of an evening with Gilbert and Sullivan. Ian found a dozen good excuses not to go out with Janet, in spite of the fact that she was looking very fetching in her new dress. They were in the kitchenette with Alan. Ian was washing-up after tea.

'You don't need me there, love,' he argued. 'I'd be an embarrassment. I'm no good at that musical stuff.'

'You don't mind it at the club,' she said.

'That's different.'

'Ian, you promised you'd come.'

'I'll make it up to you. Honest.'

'All right . . . '

Janet gave up then remembered the phone call she had taken at her mother's. Before she could tell him about it, however, there was a knock on the door. Her best friend, Annabel, had called for her on the arm of Dr Jeremy Pollock. Both were younger than Janet and as devoted as she was to the magic of Gilbert and Sullivan. The vivacious Annabel was sorry that Ian was crying off but the grinning Jeremy seemed pleased. He offered Janet his other arm.

'Oh!' she remembered, turning back to Ian. 'You had a phone call at Mum's earlier on. Somebody called Gould. About a job. Why did you give him the number of the shop when he could have spoken to you at the office?'

'Never thought of that,' said Ian.

He and Alan waved the trio off. Jeremy Pollock was in his element with an attractive woman on each arm. Janet looked over her shoulder. Ian had told her that he intended to help Alan with his homework but she had doubts. She sensed conspiracy between her menfolk.

Since their marital status had given them the right to live and work in Britain, the three French girls had gone straight into action. Hedda was on duty at the Blue Parrot when she saw Chantal moving into the shadows with an amorous naval officer. There was a brief exchange of words between them before she led him off to a private room. Claudette and Marie were also cruising the room for custom.

Hedda remained near the bar, keeping a watchful eye on all the hostesses and wondering what had happened to Dick Dobson and Ian Deasey. Their act would be sorely missed. Before she could speculate on their absence, however, two other men claimed her attention. They came into the club with long coats and serious faces. Hedda could see that they were not serviceman and wondered why they kept their coats on when they were shown to a table near the stage. She also wondered why one of them had brought a leather case.

At the Officers' Mess in Chelsea barracks, Dick and Ian were given the broom cupboard as a dressing room. They struggled to get into their dinner jackets amid the brushes and mops.

'Is my tie straight?' asked Dick.

'Tell me something,' said Ian, adjusting it for him. 'You and the wife. Have you actually . . . ?'

'Consummated?'

'Given her one?'

'Never on the first marriage.'

'Of course,' agreed Ian. 'What about you and Hedda?'

'Just good friends . . . '

Before Ian could pursue the topic, their host threw open the door and looked in with glassy eyes. Lieutenant Elwood was in uniform and he had clearly not stinted himself at the bar. A full tumbler of gin was in his hand.

'Ready chaps?' he said. 'Penguin suits on? Follow me.'

They went down the corridor after him and guessed that the rest of the audience would be in the same condition. An Officers' Mess party was no place for the temperate. When they entered the room, they got a mild jeer. The Mess was filled with regimental silver but it was dominated by a group of twenty or so junior officers, evidently competing to see who could drink most alcohol at the fastest speed. Dick and Ian noted these rowdies at once and they were disturbed.

Elwood led them on to the platform at the end of the room and Dick slipped on to the stool behind the superb Bechstein grand piano. It seemed to invite a Rachmaninov Concerto rather than the treatment he and Ian were about to give it. The rowdies started to throw food at each other and Ian was hit by a flying roll. The noise began to get out of hand until Elwood produced a revolver from inside the raised piano lid and fired it into the air.

Dick and Ian leaped with shock but the noise did the trick. Silence fell on the room and Elwood introduced his two guests.

'Gentlemen,' he announced, 'I bring you, hot-foot from the West End . . . Messrs Ian Deasey and Dick Dobson.'

The rowdies banged their fists on the tables in salute.

Ian took over. 'We have given comfort to the troops before,' he said nervously, 'but never in such splendid surroundings. I can't see why they call it a mess.'

Loud groans and cries of 'Get off' greeted the pun.

'Anyway,' he continued. 'I'd like to start with a song dedicated to Lieutenant Elwood. To remind him of his schooldays.' All eyes turned to Elwood who bowed unsteadily. Ian started. *'Bum!'* he sang.

'Tittie!' chorused the audience.

'Bum!'

'Tittie!

Ian was well and truly away now.

'Bum, bum, bum!
Don't let the soldier fire his gun, gun, gun,
He'll be waiting when you get back home
For . . . bum!'

The rowdies stamped their feet and joined in the refrain. Deasey and Dobson, both from the ranks, lowered their material to accommodate the tastes of the officers.

The two men at the Blue Parrot kept changing their drinks every time the waitress came up to serve them. Yet they never seemed to do more than sip at their glasses. They had watched the dancing troupe with offhand interest and even Hedda's erotic performance with the fans did not seem to arouse them. Marie sidled over and draped herself across the knees of one of the men but he hardly seemed to notice that she was there. Both customers remained stiff and formal. Alone of the clientele, they did not seem to be having a good time.

There were no dissenting voices at the officers' mess. Everyone thought that Deasey and Dobson were the funniest thing they had ever seen. As the songs got cruder, the choruses got louder and reached the ears of the Brigadier in another room. Thinking it was a sing-song of wartime numbers, he brought his wife to join in the fun. The junior officers parted like the Red Sea as he entered. Caught between three more bums and a tit, Ian Deasey suddenly had doubts about the suitability of their material. The Brigadier was a dignified old buffer and his wife had a smiling graciousness. To make matters worse, they were given chairs directly in front of the platform.

Dick decided they had gone too far to turn back now and he played the introduction to the next song. Ian launched himself into it with characteristic gusto.

'The Chaplain's one fixation
is sodomy, I'm sure . . .
He'll deal with deviation
When you are in form four.
It's pointless to resist him,
He does it every year.
Endeavour to assist him,
You'll get a ginger beer.'

A stony silence fell on the audience as they watched the Brigadier with apprehension. His presence was a wet blanket on the whole entertainment. Ian tried to raise a laugh by telling the senior officers, in their resplendant uniforms, that the fancy dress ball was next door. Stonier silence ensued. Dick winced and went straight into the tune of 'The British Grenadiers'. Ian sang by reflex.

> *'From the halls of Chipping Sodbury*
> *To the shores of Leigh-on-Sea,*
> *They have left their mark indelibly*
> *And it's plain for all to see.*
> *There's a cute new crop of kiddywinks,*
> *Chewing gum and wearing jeans.*
> *They're the illegitimate offspring*
> *Of the United States Marines.'*

The Brigadier guffawed and his wife shot him a look of rebuke before she, too, spluttered with mirth. The ice was broken and everyone joined in the wild laughter. They clapped in tune to the songs and cheered every new lyric.

Deasey and Dobson had triumphed.

The atmosphere at the Blue Parrot was slightly more subdued until the dancing troupe returned to the stage. Hedda did not join the act this time because she was in charge of the club in Dick's absence, and that meant hovering near the bar to supervise everything. The two men in the long coats made their way across to her.

'Is the manager here?' asked one of them.

'Not at present,' she said. 'Can I help you?'

'Inspector Wareham, Vine Street,' he said, showing her his credentials. 'And this is Mr Field, Her Majesty's Customs and Excise . . . '

To illustrate the point, Field put his case on the bar and opened it to reveal an array of glass measures and analysis kits.

'We have reason to believe,' continued Wareham, 'that you have been watering your spirits. Your whisky, your gin, your brandy, your rum . . . '

'What do you mean?' said Hedda.

'Your licence is forthwith rescinded,' he said. 'We're closing the Blue Parrot down.'

CHAPTER 7

Elated with their success in the Officer's Mess, Ian Deasey and Dick Dobson went off to change back into their civvies. They were at the rear of the stage behind the potted palms.

'Didn't I tell you, Dobson?' said Ian.

'You told me, Deasey.'

'We blitzed them!'

'We mowed them down!'

'So where do we go from here, eh?'

'Yes, where *do* we go from here?'

'Onwards and upwards,' said Ian, who had been saving the good news. 'I had a phone call from that agent. Have you ever heard of Morton Stanley?'

'Sounds like a football team.'

'Morton Stanley. The King of Variety.'

'Wouldn't know him from the Queen of Sheba.'

'We've been offered a spot,' said Ian, excitedly. 'With Morton Stanley. In Liverpool.'

'Liverpool?'

'Stand by your beds!'

Lieutenant Elwood, now almost paralytic with drink, came over to thank them. The Brigadier, his wife and the top brass suddenly bore down on them. Elwood saw the grim expressions on the hierarchy and dived for cover in the palm trees. The Brigadier's face was like an advertisement for frostbite.

'Disgraceful exhibition,' he snapped. 'Ought to be ashamed of yourselves.'

'We are, sir,' said Ian, penitentially.

'Usually get some whale of a woman, bellowin' about the White Cliffs of Dover,' said the Brigadier with a grin. 'You were a welcome change.' He indicated his wife. 'Memsahib enjoyed it very much. Well done, chaps.'

'Oh. Thank you, sir,' said Dick.

The Brigadier saw Elwood lurking among the foliage.

'You the duty officer, Elwood?'

'Yes,sir.'

'Good show. Carry on.'

Lieutenant Elwood saluted then fell forward to spew over his commander officer with spectacular accuracy.

Deasey and Dobson knew when to beat a retreat.

The motorbike took them back towards Soho and the cold night air was a tonic. Their adrenalin was still high. Dick yelled in the driver's ear above the roar of the engine.

'Get a move on!' he said. 'We may be in time to fit in our act at the Blue Parrot. It'll be open for hours yet.'

When they turned into the back-street, however, their hopes were dashed. A police van was standing outside the club and uniformed constables were escorting Chantal, Marie and Claudette into the back of it. Detective-Inspector Wareham was turning the key in a huge padlock on the door and ignoring the protests of Rudi Lorimer.

The picture told its own story. When Ian halted his machine, Hedda came over to give them more details. All three of them then adjourned to her flat for a post mortem. Dick Dobson was in a furious mood and blamed Ian Deasey.

'Every time I get involved in one of your half-baked schemes, it ends in catastrophe!'

'Steady on,' retorted Ian. 'Who helped you to elope from the Allied Officers' Club, Squadron-Leader?'

'Who got you the job at the club?'

'It wasn't a club – it was a knocking shop!'

'This is a complete disaster!' said Dick, burying his face in his hands. 'Rudi Lorimer trusted me. I let him down.'

Ian glanced at Hedda, who gave him a wry smile. Witnessing the row made her uncomfortable. Ian rallied and tried to look on the bright side.

'Cheer up, mate. There is a silver lining.'

'What?' grunted Dick.

'At least you're free to come to Liverpool.'

'I'm not going to bloody Liverpool!'

Ian was hurt. 'Then I'll go on my own.'

'Calm down, Ian,' said Hedda, softly. 'You need Dick.'

'No, I don't,' he said. 'Pianists grow on trees!'

'So do singers,' retaliated Dick. 'Go to Liverpool. I can always find a new singer. Hedda, for instance. Go on. You're on your own from now on.'

It was all over. Deasey and Dobson were divorced.

Alan Deasey packed the exercise books into his satchel then came into the kitchenette. His parents were sitting at the table over the remains of their breakfast. A sombre Ian was buried in his *Daily Mirror*.

'Can I have a lift on the motorbike, Dad?' said Alan.

'Sorry. Not today.'

Alan was disappointed but Janet signalled to him not to press his request. She gave the boy a kiss and he went out of the house, banging the door rebelliously behind him. Ian lowered his paper and felt guilty.

'I'll pick up that fishing rod today,' he said. 'For his birthday. Try to keep it as a surprise, Janet.'

'You'll be lucky,' she said. 'Alan's been talking about nothing else for the past week. Did you tell your friend about the party?'

'Yes.'

'Well? Is he coming.'

'I don't know.'

'Persuade him, if you can. Alan liked him a lot.'

Ian stood up abruptly and reached for his helmet. Dick Dobson was beyond his persuasion now. Ian had to soldier on without him.

'I'm seeing Mum at twelve,' said Janet. 'Maybe I could pop around to the office straight after?'

'No, no, love. Don't do that.'

'I've never seen where you work.'

'Oh, it's very boring,' he said. 'And I'll be tied up in this damn site meeting with Frank Parsons.'

He gave her a token kiss and crossed to the door.

'Ian,' she said, holding up his lunch box. 'You'll be needing this, if you're going to work, won't you?'

'Ah, yes . . . '

He took the box and went quickly out. Janet's face was puckered with concern as she looked after him. Something had happened but she had no idea what it could be.

Ian drove straight to the council offices and went right on past. He turned into a side-street and came to a halt beside a telephone box. Finding the number on a piece of paper, he put in his coins and dialled. He was still upset at the break-up with Dick Dobson but sentiment was not going to stand in the way of his career. The chance to appear on the same bill as Morton Stanley might be the springboard that launched him into the big time. When he was put through to the agent, he told him that he would accept the booking.

Marshall Gould shattered his illusions at once.

'You've split up?' said the dark, brown voice.

'I'm independent,' said Ian. 'Available to work on my own, Mr Gould. You know – solo.'

'Solo!' The agent made the word sound like a notifiable disease. 'As I told you, it's a chicken-and-egg situation. Except that you've just broken the egg.'

'I don't understand.'

'I want Deasey and Dobson. Morton Stanley wants Deasey and Dobson.' His voice became doom-laden. 'No Dobs: no jobs. Capisco?'

Hedda Kennedy was thrilled with the news that her husband might, after all, be alive and she asked Dick Dobson to take her to the nursing home. The now-repaired limousine scrunched over the gravel drive of a rambling half-timbered house that was set in spacious grounds. Wrapped up in dressing gowns, a few patients were sitting out in the sun in wheelchairs. Hedda was brimming with anticipation. Dick kept his fingers crossed for her. If her husband was inside the military hospital, the long journey from London would have been well worth it.

They went into the lobby to be met by Colonel Gerry Birch, a courteous American doctor who wore a white coat over his uniform. Leaving Dick behind to wait, the doctor conducted Hedda along a corridor and up some stairs. They stopped outside a room and Colonel Birch opened the door for her. Not knowing what she would find, Hedda took a deep breath and went into the room. A young man lay on the single bed against the wall. Severely burned, his hands and head were heavily bandaged and the part of his face that was visible bore terrible scars on it.

Hedda stepped forward and touched his arm lightly. If it was her husband, she wanted him back whatever condition he might be in. The man's head turned to look at her and he tried to smile. Hedda smiled back but her heart constricted.

'It's not him,' she murmured to the doctor.

'Are you sure, Mrs Kennedy?'

'Completely.'

'Sorry to have troubled you. Let me take you back.'

'No,' said Hedda. 'Do you mind if I stay for while? Just to sit with him? That can't do any harm, can it?'

'None at all,' he agreed.

The doctor went out and Hedda sat beside the bed to take the young airman's bandaged hand in her own. He was too weak to say anything but there was a faint glow of gratitude in his eyes. She stayed there for some time, wondering how she would have reacted if this really had been her husband. Hedda began to tell the patient how she and Eddie had first met and married. Talking about him seemed to help.

'Six days later,' she said, 'he was shot down over Dresden. More than two years ago now. Or, to be precise, eight hundred and thirty-four days . . . ' She gave a sad smile. 'I would have stopped looking but others in the squadron saw the crew bail out before the plane exploded. So I can't give up, can I? You hear stories all the time. Men picked up by the Russians, and not returned. Men wrongly identified. Men who lost their memories.' She sat up. 'If you knew that someone you loved was looking for you, you wouldn't say that two years was very long, would you? Not against the rest of your life.'

The door opened and the doctor returned. He tapped his watch to indicate that it was time to leave. Hedda got up and leaned over the bed to kiss the young man's forehead.

'Thank you for listening,' she said. 'Keep smiling.'

When Alan Deasey was given his star birthday present, he could not wait to try it out. His father picked him up from school that afternoon and the two of them went straight to the canal. Alan fixed his bait and proudly cast with his new fishing rod. Hook and maggots landed with a plop and the float bobbed on the surface of the dirty brown water.

'What do you think?' said Ian.

'It's a cracker, Dad. I could catch a salmon with this.'

'A pike, a shark, a white whale.' They laughed and Ian shared in his son's pleasure. 'Do you know, wherever you go in this world, you'll always meet a fellow-fisherman. Look at Jesus. First two blokes he picked, what were they doing?'

'Fishing.'

'Exactly. He developed his argument. 'And they were Jews. Eskimos fish, aborigines angle, even your desert nomad has been known to flick his flies . . . '

'How d'you fish in a desert?' asked Alan.

'At a oasis. Assuming, of course, you've got a permit.'

'Did you do it in an oasis?'

'Some of the lads did.'

'What did they catch?'

'Crabs, mainly. Very common in North Africa.'

The prefab was in silence when they got back. It had been a most successful outing and the new rod had proved its worth. Alan had caught several fish but had unhooked them all and thrown them back into the canal. They let themselves into the house and took off their wet wellingtons.

'Best birthday I've ever had,' decided Alan.

'Is it?' Ian was glad.

'You're back,' said the boy. 'Mum's happy.'

'Fish are bitin' and the cotton's high,' sang Ian. He glanced around. 'Nobody about. We've got the place all to ourselves, Alan. Let's go and sit down, shall we?'

Thrown off guard, the boy went into the living room.

'SURPRISE!'

A gang of people suddenly jumped out from behind the furniture to welcome home the birthday boy. Janet Deasey was in her new dress and Edith – by way of a perk – was wearing a new corset. Several of Alan's schoolmates had also been invited but the person he was most pleased to see was Dick Dobson. Not wishing to let the boy down, Dick had brought Hedda, whose glamorous outfit put Janet's dress in the shade.

Janet had made a birthday cake and lit the candles. As she held the cake out, Dick slipped across to the piano and played the familiar chords. Everyone sang lustily.

'Happy birthday to you,
Happy birthday to you,

Happy birthday, dear Alan,
Happy birthday to you!

With a mighty puff, Alan blew out all the candles and got a cheer. Everyone crowded around to congratulate him. Ian had been taken aback to see Dick and Hedda. He eyed them with caution. Janet stood between the two men.

'I've met your partner at long last, Ian,' she said.

'I asked him what you two get up to four nights a week.'

Ian twitched. 'You didn't tell her, did you?'

'About the goat?' said Dick. 'Of course not. Or the custard.'

'Where's that fantastic car of yours?' asked Alan.

'Hid it around the corner,' said Dick. 'Didn't want to give the game away, did I?' He handed the boy a package. 'Birthday present for you.'

'Thanks!' Alan tore off the paper and saw that he was holding a new reel for his rod. 'It's great!' He turned back to Dick. 'Did *you* ever catch crabs in the desert?'

'No, but I once had a close call in Tripoli.'

Hedda came up to be introduced and to hand a birthday card to Alan. When he opened it, he found a ten shilling note inside. He whooped with delight.

'Thanks! Thanks, Hedda!'

'Don't I get a birthday kiss?'

She gave him a smacker on the lips and the other kids screeched with mirth. Alan's cheeks were matching tomatoes.

'You're just like your father,' teased Hedda.

Janet heard the remark and caught Ian's eye.

'Right, then,' he said, uncomfortably. 'What's next?'

The cake was cut and passed around, and for a while they munched. After a few word games to get the party going, Dick urged Hedda to pay a tribute to the birthday boy. To piano accompaniment, Hedda sang with a husky sweetness.

'Smiles have been my weakness
Hearts have flipped with meekness
To the boy with the wonderful smile.
Now my search is ended,
For I've found the lad intended
After seeking many a weary smile . . . '

The rendition brought tears to Edith's eyes and she dabbed away with a handkerchief. Janet, too, was moved but Ian listened with mixed feelings. Hedda had a beautiful voice and worked well with Dick. They were a class act.

'I've been in England, Russia and France,
On Old Broadway and Main Street,
And I've had the chance
To see if someone had a smile like you, honey.
In all the world, I've never seen a smile like yours.'

Torn between embarrassment and joy, Alan settled for a kind of uneasy delight. Ian led the applause for the performance but Dick looked across at him with some misgivings. Hedda had come between the two men.

When the games resumed in earnest, the party moved out into the garden. Ian took charge and taught the kids how to play 'Was you dar?', a hilarious game which involved a duel between two blindfolded opponents who hit each other with rolled-up newspapers. Ian and Alan were the first combatants.

Janet Deasey took the opportunity to do some of the washing-up. Dick and Hedda assisted and watched the high jinks in the garden through the window.

'Alan seems to be enjoying himself,' noted Dick.

'Yes,' said Janet. 'Not as much as Ian is, though, the daft so-and-so.'

'I hope he's not too disappointed about Liverpool.'

'Liverpool?' she repeated.

'Morton Stanley and his Khaki Army.' He saw her blank face. 'I hadn't heard of them either.'

Hedda sensed trouble and tried to head him off.

'I don't think that Ian's serious about it, Dick.'

'Oh, he is,' insisted the other. 'After all, he's burned his bridges with the council.'

'Burned his bridges?' said Janet.

'Yep. Got the elbow. He's really going for showbiz now. You should have seen how he wangled us into the Chelsea Barracks bash two nights ago.'

'The Chelsea Barracks bash . . . '

The scales fell from her eyes. It was the night when Ian

had missed the Gilbert and Sullivan evening in order – he had claimed – to help Alan with his homework. Janet Deasey was shaken. She walked out of the kitchenette.

'What did I say?' asked Dick, innocently.

'You idiot!' said Hedda.

They looked through the window as Janet appeared in the garden and joined the others. Newspaper in hand, she started to belabour the blindfolded Ian unmercifully.

The party finally broke up and everyone drifted away. Ian Deasey and his wife sat opposite each other in the living room without saying a word. Alan came in, weighed up the situation at once and made a tactful withdrawal. Janet was still seething. She waited until she heard her son's bedroom door close before she spoke.

'Why didn't you tell me?' she demanded.

Ian shook his head. Words deserted him.

'I don't mind you doing those stupid shows,' she said. 'I don't mind you sneaking off to Chelsea Barracks. I don't even mind you losing your job. But not telling me!'

'Sorry, love.'

'I didn't see you for four years, but all that time I trusted you. Was I so completely wrong?'

'No,' he assured her, 'you weren't. I really am very sorry, Janet. I was in a mess.'

'You could have talked to me!'

'I know.'

'I'm not just a stupid little wifey.'

'I know, I know,' he apologized. 'When I lost my job, I just wanted to have some sort of alternative before I told you.' He leaned across. 'I'll make it up to you.'

'Oh, yeah?'

Her sigh explored a whole octave of disillusion.

Dick Dobson bounced into the Blue Parrot and found Rudi Lorimer at the bar. He gave his boss a cautious smile.

'Good evening, sir.

'Hello, Richard.'

'I knew you'd want to get things going again,' said Dick. 'Just hope it wasn't too much trouble.'

'No,' said Lorimer, calmly. 'Not for us.'

'Excellent.' His confidence returned. 'You'll be wanting the same old arrangements, I daresay? When we re-open. Yours truly, supervising the joint, tinkling the ivories.'

'The first problem is that I won't be re-opening. I have better things to do. The second problem, Richard, is that the police still have questions for the manager of the Blue Parrot. Tricky questions.'

'The manager?'

'You,' said Lorimer, casually. 'So you see, old boy, your value to me at present is somewhere around zero. Minus ten.'

Dick Dobson gulped. He left the Blue Parrot as quickly as he could and returned to his room to think things over. Marie had other plans for him. His wife was swigging wine from a bottle and cooking supper on a spirit lamp. Chantal and Claudette were reclining on his bed.

'Richard!' she said, running to embrace him.

'What the hell are you doing here?'

'We had nowhere else to go.'

'You can't stay here!'

'Yes, we can. I am your wife. You said "I do".'

'I know I did,' he confessed, 'but I don't.'

Marie switched from warm tenderness to cold brutality.

'We stay here,' she warned, 'or we go to the police and tell them everything you made us do.'

Dick felt as if he were being burned alive.

A night at the Palais de Dance made all the difference. The music was soft and the atmosphere seductive. They waltzed around the floor while a glitterball spun above their heads. Her head lay on his shoulder. Ian and Janet were like young lovers again.

'Tomorrow,' he promised, 'I'll go and see Parsons. Tell him that if he doesn't give me my job back, he'll never see your Mum's corsets again.'

She giggled. 'You're a daft sod, Ian Deasey.'

'I love you, too.'

'Well, you should show it a bit more often.'

'You asked for it,' he said, pretending to undress.

'I don't mean like that!'

'Like what?'

'Let's go home . . . '

The night was warm and a full moon guided them. They turned into their road, arm in arm, at peace with each other and with the world. Ian and Janet Deasey had at last recaptured the spirit that had brought them together in the first place.

'You won't miss it, will you?' she asked.

'Not for a second,' he said. 'It was just for laughs. And without Dick, there's not a lot of point in me trying.'

'Him and Hedda weren't at all bad together.'

'Him and me weren't at all bad.'

She kissed him. 'Never mind. I'll teach you bridge.'

He stopped to hug her when a taxi suddenly lurched towards them and screeched to a halt so close that they were forced right back on the pavement. Ian was about to protest when the hunted face of Dick Dobson emerged.

'Sorry about this, Ian,' he said, breathlessly.' But are you still on for Liverpool?'

CHAPTER 8

Like the city of Liverpool itself, Morton Stanley bore the visible scars of war. During six long years of strenuous entertaining on the Home Front, he had drunk far too much whisky, eaten far too much Yorkshire pudding and chased far too many chorus girls around the dressing rooms. Such over-indulgence leaves its mark on a man. But he was a real trouper. When he walked on to the bare stage of the Theatre Royal that Sunday morning, his spirits soared. This was home.

Morton Stanley was a short, fat, barrel-chested man in his fifties with an astrakhan coat draped over his shoulders and a Homburg hat on his head. His roly-poly face was florid and good-humoured and his eyes sparkled with youthful vitality. The stage manager saw him and gave him a deferential welcome.

'Good morning, Mr Stanley. Glad to be back in the 'pool?'

'I certainly am, Paul.'

'You always pack 'em in here.'

Morton Stanley smiled and strutted to the centre of the stage so that he could look out into the auditorium. The smile broadened into a lecherous grin when he saw a gaggle of dancing girls in the aisle.

'What a pot-pourri of pulchritude!' he said, raising his hat and moving towards them. 'Are we having trouble with our accommodation, ladies? Allow me to be of service.'

He stopped in his tracks when his wife emerged from the middle of the group. Moira Stanley was a big, brawny, hawk-eyed woman with an expression of cynicism that had been set on her face by years of marriage to Morton Stanley. Her husband's manner changed at once.

'Sorry, my dearest. I didn't see you there.'

'*I* can manage the ladies' digs,' she said, pointedly. 'There's no need for you to butt into them, Morton.'

She flicked her fingers and the girls scampered off to the dressing rooms, throwing nods and smiles to him as they went past. He threw a wistful glance after them then joined his wife in the auditorium.

'Anything I can do to assist you, sweetness?' he said.

'Have you checked our old room at the Adelphi?'

'Just as it always is – even down to the bomb damage.'

'Good.' Moira Stanley was peremptory. 'I think you should open with your Herman the German number, and finish with 'Dear Old Donegal'. They're all Irish up here and totally undiscriminating.' She sniffed. 'They'll love you.'

Morton Stanley gazed at her with an amalgam of fear and fondness which had kept him chained to her for forty years.

'Where would I be without you, Moira?' he said.

'Dead of the clap.' She looked round. 'Where on earth are those damn ice-breakers?'

It was raining heavily as Ian Deasey and Dick Dobson drove towards Liverpool on the motorbike. A lorry roared past them, its hissing tyres sending up a deluge of rainwater. The motorbike surfed for another fifty yards then pulled up outside a concrete pillbox. The two men leapt off the machine and raced for cover. Inside the pillbox, they found some old wooden boxes and oily rags. They lit a fire then stripped off their wet things and stood in their underpants. Ian took out a small bottle of whiskey and had a swig.

'It stinks in here,' he said.

'I noticed.'

'I hope Morton Stanley appreciates this.'

'Yes, we're making all this effort for him.' Dick took the proffered bottle and drank from it. 'That's the spirit!'

'So what are we going to do?' said Ian.

'Dry out and wait till the rain stops.'

'On stage, I mean. Our act.'

'Don't ask me, mate. I'm only the piano-player.'

'We could rehearse something now.'

'Juggling?' suggested Dick, lobbing the bottle to Ian.

'Or fire-breathing,' said Ian, spitting a mouthful of whisky on to the flames to make them roar.

'What about ventriloquism?'

'I'm not sitting on your knee for *anything*!' said Ian. 'Wait, I've got it! The Sand Dance!'

He went into a demonstration and Dick chortled at his hieroglyphic movements before taking over the choreography.

'Tap dance!' ordered Dick and his partner obeyed at once. 'Morris dance!' Ian began a rural skip. 'Ballet dance!' He did *grands jetés* across the fire. Dick was in hysterics by now. 'Irish jig!'

Ian obliged once more with vigour, singing 'Dear Old Donegal' at the top of his voice and dancing as if the seat of his underpants were on fire. At the height of the performance, he lost his footing and fell heavily on his backside. He sat in a pile of filth and his nose twitched.

'I've fallen in something nasty,' he said.

'That's showbiz for you!'

They were both convulsed with laughter but the horseplay did yield a positive result. As Ian hauled himself up again, inspiration suddenly came to him.

'Wait!' he said. 'I've got a wonderful idea!'

Janet Deasey poured out the cups of tea then handed around the scones. She had invited Jeremy Pollock and Annabel to join them that Sunday afternoon. Edith, as alert and smart as usual, was in one of the armchairs while a bored Alan sat in the other. He hated being clucked over by his mother and grandmother, and grinned at by Annabel. The war had almost suffocated him with female company. He wanted his father.

Annabel wolfed one of the home-made scones.

'I didn't see Ian in church this morning,' she said.

'That's because he wasn't there,' said Edith.

'No,' added Janet. 'He's . . . gone off with a friend.'

'To Liverpool,' said Alan, tired of the way adults never told the truth. 'Dad's appearing with Morton Stanley at the theatre there. Song and dance act.'

'That's very enterprising,' observed Pollock.

'Thank you, Alan,' said Janet, shooting him a reproving glance. 'Let's not talk about that just now.'

'What a pity!' said Pollock. 'I've been given a couple of extra tickets for Palestrina tomorrow, and I was going to offer them to you and Ian.'

Janet was pleased but not at all sure whether she ought accept the offer. Edith pounced swiftly on the opportunity.

'Well, I say, that does sound very nice, Dr Pollock. How kind! You must go, Janet.'

'Will you come with me, Mum?'

'Ah, well,' said Edith evasively, 'I've got a friend coming round for tea tomorrow night.'

'The concert won't start till late,' said Pollock.

'Neither will the tea . . . Take Alan.'

'No, thanks,' he said quickly.

'Say yes, or I'll break your arm,' joked Pollock in his bedside manner voice. 'That's settled. Good man.'

'We'll be pleased to come, Jeremy,' said Janet.

'Lovely to have you.'

She got up and went into the kitchenette to make another pot of tea. Alan popped his head around the door.

'What's Palestrina?' he whispered.

'I think it's some sort of cheese.'

Edith came into the kitchenette to replenish the empty plate with scones. Rain was lashing at the windows. She rid herself of another moan about her son-in-law.

'What's he trying to prove, Janet?'

'I wish I knew.'

'First the war. Now Liverpool. He's unreliable.'

'He'll be back in three weeks,' said Alan.

'And the war wasn't his fault, Mum.'

'It was a good excuse, though, wasn't it?' said Edith harshly. 'And now they won't grow up. None of them.' She looked at the weather. 'And how am I going to get home? It's piddling down. I'm trapped here but I bet Ian and that friend of his are lording it up somewhere posh.'

The concrete pillbox had been an unsatisfactory resting place. Rain had seeped into the motorbike and they had been unable to start it. Forced to sleep rough in their fetid cabin, Ian and Dick emerged stiffly into the daylight like a pair of tramps. They managed to get the motorbike going and headed for Liverpool as fast as they could. They stank like a over-crowded dog kennel. By the time they pulled up outside the Royal Theatre, they were thoroughly jaded.

Ian then spotted something and revived slightly.

'Look!' he said. 'There we are!'

'Where?'

'There!

Ian jabbed a finger at one of the playbills which had been posted up. MORTON STANLEY'S BARMY ARMY — BEATING THE RETREAT was emblazoned at the top in large letters, with the supporting acts arranged in boxes below. Their own names were in the smallest type of all in a box shaped uncomfortably like a coffin, but they were pleased nevertheless. Deasey and Dobson had made it.

They went into the theatre to find the stage manager standing on a ladder in the foyer to replace a light bulb.

'Can I help you, gentlemen?' he said.

'Yes,' said Dick, grandly. 'Would you inform Mr Stanley that Messrs Deasey and Dobson have arrived.'

'You mean that *you* are Deasey and Dobson?'

'That's right,' they said in unison.

'Well, you should have been here yesterday lunchtime.'

'Spot of mechanical trouble,' said Dick.

'If I were you,' advised the stage manager, 'I'd get your arse into the auditorium double quick. He's doing a run-through.' He pointed a light bulb. 'Through there. It's a great big room with a lot of seats.'

They went through the double doors into the rear of the auditorium. The house lights were down but the working lights were up on the stage. Morton Stanley was rehearsing a lacklustre chorus line, watched from the auditorium by his vigilant wife. The girls were in mufti and their director was standing on stage in front of them, trying to whip some life into the joyless routine.

'And . . . one, two, three,' he encouraged. 'And one, two, three. Put some effort into it, girls! For pity's sake!'

The newcomers were less than impressed by it all.

'I've seen better at the Blue Parrot,' said Dick.

'Yes,' said Ian. 'Hey, that's him. Morton Stanley.'

'Which one?'

'The one in the trousers, idiot.'

The pianist brought the number to an end and the girls tap-danced untidily off into the wings. Stanley watched them go like a man watching his luxury yacht sink.

'That was bloody awful!' he said.

'Do it again, then,' ordered Moira.

'No, my dove. What do you expect for one and a kick? The Bolshoi Ballet?' He needed resuscitation. 'Paul!'

The stage manager appeared magically from the wings with a glass of whisky in his hand. Stanley drank it down.

'Deasey and Dobson have arrived,' said Paul.

'The bailiffs?'

'The openers,' said Moira.

'The murder slot!' Morton Stanley peered out into the gloom of the auditorium. 'Where are you skulking? Show yourselves!'

Ian and Dick came forward a little shamefaced.

'Good afternoon, Mr Stanley,' said Ian.

'Sorry we're late. Unforeseen hold-up.'

Morton Stanley got their measure in a second. They did not inspire him. He turned away and left them to his wife.

'Dressing room thirteen,' said Moira, crisply. 'You've missed your rehearsal slot. Your half's at five twenty-five and I'll knock this morning off your wages. Evening show, six sharp.'

Ian was baffled. 'Our half?'

'Half what?' asked Dick.

'God help us!' groaned Moira. 'Half an hour, dear. The half an hour you need to be here before the show starts or we sack you.' She rolled her eyes. 'Is it worth waiting till half-past five, I ask myself? . . .Where are your band parts?'

'We don't have a band.'

'So what do you want to come on to?'

'Applause will do,' said Ian hopefully.

Morton Stanley went off into a peal of false laughter.

'Let's hope you're that funny tonight,' said Moira.

'We will be,' promised Ian. 'See you later.'

'Yes,' said Dick, 'at our half.'

They walked off and the Stanleys traded a knowing look.

'Old soldiers never die!' said Moira.

Her husband grimaced. 'They only smell that way.'

The choir sang by candlelight and the music of Palestrina soared into the nave of the church. Janet Deasey and Alan sat near the front of the audience with Jeremy Pollock and Annabel. The doctor was entranced by the performance but

Alan and Annabel were bored stiff. Janet knew little about choral music but she was held in rapture throughout. When the choir reached the end of a section, there was an appreciative murmur along the pews.

Jeremy Pollock gave Annabel a sharp nudge.

'Still awake?'

'Beast!'

'When Palestrina wrote the *Stabat Mater*,' he said, 'he hadn't eaten for a week. He sold the manuscript to his patron for a bowl of gruel and a blanket.'

'Didn't they have ration cards?' said Alan.

'It was beautiful, Jeremy,' said Janet.

Her son betrayed her. 'You thought Palestrina was a sort of cheese.'

An embarrassed pause gave way to laughter. They were hissed into silence by neighbours as the choir began again.

The show at the Theatre Royal that evening got off to a less-than-rousing start with the dancers, in sequined sailor suits, leg-kicking unevenly through 'Anchors Aweigh'. A nervous Ian Deasey and Dick Dobson waited in the wings, wearing threadbare military greatcoats and forage caps. Ian had stuck on a Hitler moustache. They were totally eclipsed by the magnificent uniform of Morton Stanley, who was like a generalissimo from a comic opera. As the curtains closed, Stanley took a glass from the stage manager and downed it in a gulp before handing it to Ian and going out on stage. He twirled to show off his costume.

'What do you think of it, then?' Cat-calls and wolf-whistles came from a lively audience. 'Got it from Goering. Remember, dear? Herman the German. A memorable evening of strip poker in Potsdam. I had the bugger right down to his unterden lindens. Not a pretty sight, madam, believe me . . .' The audience loved him. He spoke in pukka Scouse. 'But it's great to be back in the 'pool!' He reverted to his normal bang-it-out delivery. 'So have we got a wonderful evening lined up for you? . . . Sadly no!' Chuckles all round. 'Not so much a roll of honour as a casualty list. And the first over the top – two of the walking wounded, recently returned from daring deeds in the desert – Dobson and Deasey!'

'Deasey and Dobson,' complained Ian in the wings.

'Break a leg,' said Dick.

The band played Morton Stanley off and a few bars from the Desert Song got the openers on. Both of them froze. This was no drunken audience of officers but a critical paying audience who knew what they liked. Dick sat at the piano with trembling hands above the keys. Ian was using an upturned brush as a crutch and kept one leg bent right up to suggest he had lost it. His voice was a distant croak.

'Speak up!' yelled the first heckler.

Dick played 'It's A Long Way to Tipperary' and they sang alternate lines. The ordeal began in earnest.

'It's a long way to old New Brighton
It's a long way to Skeg
It's a long way from here to Huyton
When you've only got one peg
. . . Leg!
Goodbye, playing rudies
Farewell carnal sin
'Cause you can't get your leg across a Judy
When you've only got – one pin!'

Mute horror gave way to loud abuse and the audience heckled wildly as the duo went unwisely into a second tastless verse. They plumbed new depths of failure. Dick played, Ian hopped on one leg and Morton Stanley hugged himself with glee in the wings.

'Die, you bastards!' he said, cackling. 'Die!'

After the church concert, the four of them sat in Pollock's car to eat fish and chips. Janet was beside him in the passenger seat. He teased her about Palestrina cheese and she prodded him playfully. Annabel scolded her boyfriend.

'You're a brute, Jeremy.'

'That's what you like about me, darling.'

'That and your fish and chips.' They all laughed. 'We used to talk about nothing but food during the war, didn't we, Jan?' A fruity giggle. 'Well, food and the other thing.'

'What's the other?' asked Alan.

'It's a sort of meat,' said Janet.

'Was it rationed?'

The adults laughed and the car rocked. Alan frowned.

'You couldn't get very much of it during the war,' said his mother, 'Nor afterwards, as it turns out.'

'It's very nutritional,' said Pollock, enjoying the excuse to nudge Janet. 'Perhaps they'll have it on the National Health.'

The adults sniggered and Alan felt left out.

'In the absence of the other,' said Pollock, offering a chip to Janet, 'have a Beethoven.'

'Thanks.'

'We must do this again some time.'

She chewed daintily. 'Yes, Jeremy . . . '

Morton Stanley brought the show to a thunderous conclusion by conducting a sing-song of 'Dear Old Donegal'. A dapper man in reality, he was larger-than-life on stage and he knew exactly how to maintain control. Pointing to the names on the huge song-sheet, he got a largely Irish audience into a frenzy of patriotism that ended in a huge ovation. Ian and Dick watched from the wings with a bewildered disgust.

'How the hell does he do it?' said Ian.

The curtains closed and the whole cast shuffled on to take their bow. As the tabs opened, Morton Stanley's bulk was placed in front of the two friends and largely obscured them. The baying patrons were standing up to cheer and shout. Morton Stanley's genius had piloted the show succesfully through.

Dick stared out at them with weary indifference.

'Appalling! Why don't they all go to the cinema?'

He and Ian were the first off, slinking away to their dressing room to hide from the shame of it all. Their act had been ill-chosen and badly-performed. They now had some idea what crucifixion was all about. Changing swiftly, Ian left the theatre by the stage door and a knot of autograph-hunters surged forward. When they recognized him, there was a communal groan. He walked hurriedly past but one spectator caught up with them.

'May *I* have your autograph?' said Hedda, looking more glamorous than ever in a fur-collared coat. She applauded with gloved hands. 'You were terrible.'

'What are *you* doing here?' he asked.

'Came to see you, of course.'

'Why?'

Hurt by the unfriendly question, Hedda hit right back.

'Well, I think you're going to need some professional advice, for a start.'

'What – from a Blue Parrot chorus girl?' he said with withering scorn. 'Save your breath. We're fine, thanks.'

And he turned his back on her and walked away.

CHAPTER 9

The Lord Nelson pub adjoined the theatre and acted as its overflow valve. Dick Dobson and Ian Deasey met up at the bar and kept their heads down for fear of being spotted by vengeful members of the audience. They were surprised when they overheard praise from two Liverpool dockers nearby.

'What about the show tonight, then?' said one.

'Brilliant, mate,' said the other. 'Laughed like a drain.'

'Laugh? I nearly swallowed my teeth. Fantastic!'

'That Morton Stanley. Pure class.' And the rest of 'em. Bloody great!'

Dick was so delighted that he turned to speak to them.

'You would have seen us, then – Deasey and Dobson.'

The dockers looked at him with undisguised contempt.

'Of course, some of the acts were crap,' said one.

They howled derisively. Dick and Ian writhed in agony. Their professional debut had won them no friends but many enemies. A sudden hush fell on the bar and they turned to see what had caused it. Hedda Kennedy had just entered and was posing in the doorway like a model out of *Reveille.* When she saw them, she came over to receive a welcoming hug from Dick Dobson.

'Hedda!' he said. 'Oh, Angel of Mercy. What on earth are you doing in Liverpool?'

'Your wife ran out of money and took in paying guests.'

'What! In my flat?'

'And mine – when I wasn't around.'

'Oh, no! Oh, dear!'

'That's what the police said. So I came north to rest my nerves.'

'Stay away from the Theatre Royal, then.'

'Too late, I'm afraid.' Dick shoved Ian off a bar stool so

that she could sit down. 'I thought I'd cheer you on.'

'We didn't hear you, did we, Ian?'

'I was somewhat outnumbered.' She tried to be positive. 'Well, it can only get better. What shall we have to celebrate?'

'How about morphine?' said Ian, ruefully.

Dick ordered gins all round as Morton Stanley passed.

'Mine's a large scotch,' said the star of the show as he headed for the gents. 'Got to see a man about a dog.'

When the gins were poured, Dick paid. A glass of whisky was then plonked down on the counter in front of Ian.

'Five bob,' said the barman.

'How much!' gulped Ian.

'Triple black label. Mr Stanley's regular order.'

Ian paid up reluctantly. Morton Stanley breezed in again and swept up the drink with a flabby smile.

'Very decent of you . . . er . . . '

'Deasey . . . Ian.'

'Deasey Ian.' He saw Hedda and beamed. 'And what have we here?' Dick introduced them and he kissed Hedda's hand with exaggerated courtesy. 'Charmed, my dear.' He glanced at the two men. 'Did you witness the debacle?'

'They did their best,' she said, loyally.

'Indeed,' agreed Morton Stanley. 'We all have to start somewhere. Never say die – even though they did!' He looked at his watch. 'Time's up. The missus will be yowling for my firm body.' He swallowed the drink in one draught then appraised Hedda more carefully. 'Shall we be seeing more of you?'

'That depends on my friends,' she said.

'Let's hope they're not lynched tomorrow night, then,' he said with a harsh giggle. 'Toodle pip.'

Hedda watched Morton Stanley sweep out of the bar to mild applause. Dick Dobson thought of the practicalities.

'Where are you staying tonight?' he asked.

Hedda turned large, innocent, appealing eyes on them but Ian held his hands up and shook his head violently.

'Oh no you're not!'

Edith Cooper had just finished arranging a new window display at her corsetry shop when her daughter arrived. Mouth still full of pins, Edith led her into the kitchen at the rear of the premises.

It was morning and she had not yet opened up for business. Janet Deasey was an early bird in search of severely rationed worms.

'Anything I can get you, Mum?' she asked. 'I want to be first at the butcher's or I'll miss all the best cuts.'

Edith took the pins from her mouth and pondered.

'See if they've got any kidney,' she said.

'Right.'

'By the way, how was that sing-song last night?'

'Do you mind!' said Janet with dignity. 'It was a recital of Renaissance church music.'

Edith raised a mocking eyebrow. 'We *are* moving in extended circles? Thought that young Doctor was Annabel's catch.'

'He is, Mum.'

'Then he's spoken for, is he?'

'Yes,' said Janet firmly. 'And so am I.'

'Not a case of "When the cat's away", then?'

'The cat was away for four years,' reminded her daughter. 'How much kidney did you want?'

'Half a pound?'

'Isn't that rather a lot?'

'Not for two.' She continued quickly. 'I like to put a bit by for Mrs Moult. Poor soul doesn't get much.'

Janet was about to draw a vulgar parallel with her own position but she thought better of it. Edith's mind was also running on the shortcomings of Ian Deasey.

'Can you trust him up there, Janet?'

'Up where?'

'Liverpool.'

'Of course, Mum. He's pursuing his new career.'

'As long as that's all he's pursuing,' said Edith. 'You know what those variety shows are like. Full of temptation.'

'Not for him.'

'He's a man, isn't he? Separated from his wife. Off the leash.' She wagged a finger. 'How do you know that he isn't sharing a room with a chorus-girl right now?'

Janet laughed. The idea was ridiculous.

Ian Deasey dreamed that he was lying in his wife's arms then awoke to find that her face had grown two unsightly feet during the night. He realized with a start that he was lying top to toe with Dick Dobson in a narrow single bed. Despite his objections, his own bed had been surrendered to Hedda Kennedy, who was still asleep the other side of the curtain which they had rigged up. Dick had smuggled her in past the superhuman hearing of the landlady, Mrs O'Callaghan, by the simple device of carrying Hedda on his back.

'What day is it?' said Ian.

'Liverpool,' replied Dick.

'Was last night really as bad as I remember it?'

'Worse!'

Ian stood up to peer over the curtain at Hedda. She looked gorgeous in a silk nightdress and was just stirring.

'Mr Deasey!' called the landlady outside the door.

'Just a moment, Mrs O'Callaghan!' he said in a panic. 'Quick, Hedda! You'll have to hide!'

'Where?'

'She mustn't find you here!'

As he leaned on the curtain, it fell beneath his weight and he landed beside her on the bed at the precise moment that the landlady barged in. Mrs O'Callaghan was a stern woman of middle years with a Catholic insistence on moral proprieties among her lodgers. She pointed at Hedda.

'Who is this lady?' she demanded.

'That's no lady,' said Dick, smoothly. 'That's his wife.'

Ian baulked. 'What?'

'You're Mrs Deasey?' said the landlady with suspicion.

'That's right,' said Hedda, holding up her wedding ring for inspection. 'I'm Hedda Deasey.'

'What?' Ian reeled again.

'That's all right, then,' said Mrs O'Callaghan, easily. 'Breakfast's ready. I'll set a place for you, love.'

The landlady went out and Ian accosted his friends.

'What?' he demanded.

'Stop saying that!' complained Dick. 'A lot of men would give their eye teeth to be married to Hedda.'

She rose from the bed, pulled back the curtains and stretched languorously. Picking up her sponge bag, she asked if she could use the bathroom first then glided out.

Ian was still deeply upset by her arrival.

'What's she here for?' he said.

'To give us moral support.'

'We didn't ask for it.'

'We bloody need it!' said Dick. 'Besides . . . '

'Yes?'

'Hedda wanted you. She misses her husband.'

Morton Stanley stood at the rear of the auditorium and watched Deasey and Dobson trying to resurrect their act with the help of Hedda. The sight of her figure in a tight-fitting dress made Stanley's eyes water. His wife materialized behind him.

'Too wet for golf, was it?' she said.

'It was, my pet,' he replied. 'Rained so much, the members were having lifeboat drill in the clubhouse.'

'Lucky you had something to occupy you here.'

'Yes. Work, work, work! I'm a stickler for keeping a fatherly eye on my artistes.'

'Watching her wiggle when she walks, you mean?'

'My petal,' he cooed. 'It's Deasey and Dobson. There's a lot of talent up on that stage.'

'I can see her,' grunted Moira. 'What's her name?'

Unaware that she was under surveillance, Hedda Kennedy was doing her best to help her friends. Dick was glad of any assistance but Ian was clearly irritated.

'What about a hornpipe?' he suggested. 'How does it go?'

'They do a little hop,' said Hedda.

'Who do?'

'Sailors.' Dick played a hornpipe on the piano and Hedda danced expertly. 'It's all based on nautical tasks. They pull a rope. They hop. They launch a boat.'

'Then they all die of scurvy,' said Ian scornfully. 'What is this? The Spithead bloody Review?'

'I'm only trying to help,' she said.

'Well, go and help somebody else. You'd be all the rage in Borneo or somewhere tropical.'

Dick played and sang to cover an awkward moment.

'I'm . . . putting on my top hat,
Tyin' up my white tie . . . '

'Leaning on my crutch!' said a melancholy Ian.

'It's an idea.'

'No, it isn't.'

'We could always go back to "Bum Titty".'

'In front of *that* audience? Are you mad!' He scratched his head. 'Hold up. What was that thing we did last Christmas?' He sang to the tune of 'I'll Take You Home Again Kathleen'. *'I'll take my trousers down, Kathleen . . .'*

'And give you such a bloody shock,' continued Dick.

'It was a wow!'

'Are you sure?'

'We must work it into the act, Dick.'

'I have my doubts.'

'Trust me,' said Ian. 'It's a sure-fire winner.'

Deasey and Dobson were thrown before a live audience that evening for the second time and they came to see their debut in a more favourable light. During the first show, they were merely heckled and booed. This time they came in for of missiles as well. The peg-leg routine fell as flat as a pancake and the folly of besmirching a much-loved Irish song before Irish spectators was soon demonstrated. Morton Stanley was rocking with mirth in the wings as Deasey and Dobson came running off to dodge the abuse.

Dick was mortified. 'Any more brilliant ideas?'

'Yes,' said Ian. 'How about going home?'

When the show was over, Dick went straight off to the bar to revive himself but Ian stayed in the dressing room. Morton Stanley let himself in for a quiet chat.

'The crutch has got to go,' he said.

'You reckon?'

'We've had complaints.'

'Oh.'

'Don't be depressed. Might be the best performance you ever give.' He offered token pity. 'You've got a Naafi act. They're two-a-penny. Moira will have you out unless you come up with something better. You'll get there in the end.'

Ian was glum. 'Really think so?'

'Yes. You remind me of a partner I once had.'

'What happened to him?'

'He got a better offer.'

'Who from?'

'St Peter. He got run down by a bus.'

'I think I've heard this one before . . . '

'Have you?' said Stanley. 'It was in the Fulham Road.'

'Oh.' Ian realized his boss was being serious. 'Sorry.'

'Don't be. It was the funniest thing he ever did.'

Ian laughed nervously, demoralized by his own failure and over-awed by the success of Morton Stanley. There was a knock on the door and Moira came sailing in.

'Hello, my poppet,' said her husband. 'Just giving our young friend some advice.'

'How about – Australia's lovely at this time of the year?' she said then went out again. 'Turn off the lights when you go. It saves money.'

'Where was I?' said Stanley. 'Ah, yes. My mate. We had this marvellous act. I could let you have it.'

'Me!' Ian was flattered. 'That'd be great. What was it?'

'I'll show you.' He dipped his finger in the tin of removing cream and drew a diagram on the mirror. 'You've got the stage here, see, and the circle . . . ' He broke off. 'Damn! I forgot. You need a woman for the act.'

'A woman?'

'A singer. Tits and tonsils.'

'What about one of the chorus?'

'Please!' said Stanley with disdain. 'Kicking their legs in the air already overheats their brains.'

'Should we advertise?'

'What in – the *Dockers' Gazette*? You haven't got all year, matey. You want someone now. Any ideas?'

'Well,' said Ian, casting around, 'I suppose that we could, as a stop-gap, try Hedda.'

'That blonde tart? We can't use your scrubber, Deasey.'

'She's not my scrubber!'

'Can she sing?'

'Very well.'

'Better have a look at her.'

'I'll tell Hedda.'

'Damn!' said Morton Stanley, pretending that he had only just realized something. 'Double damn! It's wages. The missus won't have another body on the payroll – especially a body like Hedda's.'

'Oh, well, maybe we could pay her out of our cut.'

'Yes,' said Stanley, 'But won't your partner mind?'

'No, no,' lied Ian. 'He won't mind.'

☆ ☆ ☆

When Janet Deasey went into her son's bedroom next morning to wake him up, she got a shock. Alan was covered in spots. She told him to stay where he was and rushed around to her mother's shop to use the telephone. Dr Jeremy Pollock made the prefab his first house-call that day and he confirmed Janet's own diagnosis.

'Chicken pox,' he said. 'Not very pleasant but hardly terminal. Keep him off school for a week.'

'Thanks!' Alan grinned spottily.

'Stay in the warm, young man. Plenty of fluids.'

Janet went out into the hall with the doctor.

'What about you?' he asked.

'I feel fine.'

'I meant, have you ever had chicken pox yourself?'

'Oh, yes . . . I think so.'

'And Ian?'

'I'm not sure.

'You'd better warn him,' said Pollock. 'Chicken pox is very infectious and it can be much worse for adults.' She nodded. 'Right, then, I'll call in again later on.'

'Is that necessary, doctor?'

'No,' he said with a grin, 'but it will be a good excuse to see you again.' He became serious. 'It's none of my business, but I think Ian's mad to leave you, even for a day.'

'As you say, it's none of your business,' said the anxious Janet, taking out a handkerchief. 'He's thirty-six and he's run away to join a bloody circus!' She blew her nose to hide her emotions. 'I'm sorry. Thanks for coming.'

'My pleasure. Take care of yourself.'

Ian Deasey took the phone call from his wife and assured her that he was not at risk. He had had chicken pox as a child. A tearful Janet asked him to come home but he told that her that he had to persevere even though their act had so far been a disaster.

'I can't let Dick down. He's set his heart on this.'

'Right,' said Janet, 'until you decide that your wife and sick son are more important than Dick, you'd better stay away!'

She slammed down the receiver on him. Ian sighed.

Chicken pox took second place to the more immediate problem of soothing Dick Dobson. Ready to incorporate

Hedda into the act, he drew the line at sharing his meagre pittance with her and had a fierce argument over the matter with Ian. Dick eventually came to see that, without Hedda, he might soon have no wages at all. Compromise was needed. They rehearsed hard all day and tried the new act out that evening.

It was a revelation. Instead of being confronted with a one-legged soldier, the audience saw a glamorous young woman in a slinky dress. As Dick played, Hedda sang a music hall favourite with great feeling.

'The boy I love is up in the gallery,
The boy I love is looking down at me . . . '

With the band joining in, she had the spectators in the palm of her hand. Her voice lulled them into a mood which was immediately shattered by the appearance in the gallery of Ian Deasey as a Jolly Jack Tar. He responded with shouts and waves, falling over the audience in his anxiety to get to his beloved who was singing about him. As a comic routine, it was simple and corny but they adored it. By the time, he had shinned down a rope to join Hedda on stage, the audience was in fits of laughter. Deasey and Dobson got something they had never expected to hear in Liverpool – ecstatic applause.

They opened a bottle in the dressing room to celebrate.

'I hate to say this, Deasey,' admitted Dick,' but I thought you were damned funny tonight.'

'So did I,' said Hedda. 'When you fell in the orchestra pit at the end, I thought you'd broken your neck.'

'It felt as if I did.'

'All in all,' said Dick, 'we were a hit.'

'Does that mean I'm hired?' said Hedda.

Ian sighed. 'We don't have much choice.'

'Thanks very much!'

'I didn't mean it like that, Hedda.'

'Well, that's what it sounded like.'

'Sorry,' he said with evident sincerity. 'You saved us. We're glad to have you. Welcome to Deasey and Dobson!'

'Dobson and Deasey,' corrected Dick.

Ian gave her an affectionate peck on the cheek. She was so pleased that she responded by with a full kiss on the lips.

'Careful!' said Dick in alarm. 'Ian's married.'

'Yes,' she said. 'To me.'

Joined together on stage, they still remained apart in the bedroom. While the men endured another night of top-to-toe slumber, Hedda had a bed to herself behind the curtain. She awoke early to hear the sound of wild scratching.

'What are you two up to?' she called out.

'This bed's got fleas,' said Dick, scratching madly.

Ian sat up to look at him and yelled out. Hedda peered over the curtain to see what the problem was. Both she and Ian then backed away in horror.

Dick Dobson's face was a mass of ugly red spots.

CHAPTER 10

When Dick Dobson saw himself in the bathroom mirror, he flew into a panic convinced that he had an incurable disease. He took to his bed at once and demanded medical attention. Needing their pianist for the performance, Ian and Hedda tried to persuade him that he merely had a rash, which could be covered by stage make-up. But Dick moaned on and they finally relented. A doctor was called. He took the patient's temperature and gave him a cursory examination. Dick clutched neurotically at the man's sleeve.

'Don't leave me, Doctor,' he pleaded. 'I'm dying.'

'Stop arsing about,' said Ian. 'There's nothing really wrong with you. He can get up now, can't he, Doctor?'

'No,' said the medic.

'This man's got a matinee and an evening performance. His public expect it of him.'

'He's not going anywhere near the public,' said the doctor, categorically. 'Mr Dobson has chicken pox. He's highly infectious.'

'You've hardly looked at him.'

'I've got eyes, Mr Deasey. Your friend has got to be quarantined.'

'Yes,' insisted Dick. 'I should be in hospital.'

'I'm not having you spread your bacteria around the rest of my patients,' said the doctor. 'A separate room here will be adequate. You're not to be moved for a week.'

'A week!' wailed Ian. 'What do I tell Morton Stanley?'

Morton Stanley was in the Turkish bath, telling anecdotes to his stage manager and giving him instructions about the next performance. Both men were swathed in towels and running with perspiration. Stanley lapsed briefly into song.

'She was only a fishmonger's daughter
But she lay on a slab and said "fillet".'

Ian Deasey had been told where to find his employer. Dressed in his suit, he groped his way through the mist.

'Deasey!' said Morton Stanley.

'I need to have a private word.'

'Get your kecks off. Don't mind us.'

'It is a bit warm in here,' agreed Ian, taking off his coat and undoing his tie. 'Now, then – it's Dick.'

'Isn't it always!' said his boss with a sigh.

'Dick Dobson. He's ill. Chicken pox. He can't perform for a week. What do we do?'

Crises were a daily event in Morton Stanley's life and he knew how to handle them. Beckoning Ian after him, he went into the changing room and swabbed himself with a towel.

'Best thing that could've happened to you,' he said.

'What?'

'Losing Dobson. Piano players, two-a-penny.'

'But we've been together since . . . '

'Since the desert, I can imagine. So what, Ian? All he does is doodle at the joanna. Anyone can do that.'

Ian wanted to defend his partner but the words would not come. He began to see the sense in what Morton Stanley was saying, even though he was a little shocked at the ease with which he found himself betraying Dick.

'He doesn't really like the theatre.'

'There you go, then,' said his boss. 'I saw you, hopping round in that God-awful act, and I saw something of myself as a young man. Energy. Ideas. Stupidity.' He gripped Ian's shoulder. 'If you're tough enough, ambitious enough and make the right decisions, you can go all the way, Ian. You've got a big future ahead of you.'

'What about the two performances today?'

'You're going to work with me.'

'With you?' Ian was bowled over.

'The amputation routine. Works like a charm.'

'Is that the one you were telling me about?'

'Yes,' said Stanley. 'Trust me. I know what works. Look at the way I transformed Deasey and Dobson. This act is even better than that.'

'I'm honoured,' said Ian. 'Just the two of us?'

'We need a nurse with a pair of legs.'

'Hedda would be perfect.'

'There's more to this than bloody warbling.'

'I'm sure she can do it.'

'Well, all right,' said Stanley, 'we'll give her a try. But you've got to be guided by your head, Deasey, not by your trousers.'

Ian was affronted. 'I'm a married man!'

'So am I, matey,' said his boss, knowingly. 'So am I.'

The waiting room at the surgery was full when Janet Deasey arrived and she resigned herself to a long sit. When Jeremy Pollock came out of his consulting room and saw her, however, he summoned her straight in. She was very self-conscious about having jumped the queue.

'You really shouldn't do this,' she said.

'Ointment for Alan.' He handed her a tin.

'I should have waited my turn in there.'

'Apply it at night. It'll help him sleep.'

'Thank you, Doctor.' She moved to the door.

'Sit!' he ordered in his professional voice.

'Don't talk to me like that.'

'Sorry, Janet.' He waved her to the chair. 'Please sit down for a moment.' She looked guiltily towards the waiting room. 'No-one's going to die. I have a proposition for you.'

She hovered over the chair then finally sat on it.

'A proposition?'

'I need help. I can't organize my way out of a paper bag. You've seen what it's like out there. It's because I lost my diary and double-booked all my appointments.'

'But I've had no experience as a receptionist.'

'You're efficient,' he said. 'Annabel has told me how you ran things during the war. And I've seen how you've managed Alan. Would you consider taking a job here?'

Janet was surprised, pleased but very uncertain.

'Is this sensible, Doctor?'

'Very sensible.'

'What about Annabel?'

'You're Annabel's best friend. I value that.'

'Yes, of course . . . '

His eyes devoured her hungrily and she found the

intensity of his gaze unsettling. At the same time, it was a handsome offer and a regular wage would be useful if Ian intended to work in such a precarious profession. Jeremy Pollock could see her vacillation. He leaned forward.

'Will you at least think about it. Please?'

'Yes.' She stood up. 'How much for the ointment?'

He smiled. 'We'll talk about that another time . . . '

Dick Dobson was sitting up in bed, reading the *Liverpool Echo* and smoking a cigarette when Mrs O'Callaghan tapped on the door. The landlady carried a tray on which two glasses and two bottles of Guinness were set.

'Are you decent?' she asked, coming straight in.

'Hello, Mrs O'C.'

'How are you feeling, luvvie?'

'Bearing up.'

'Brought you something to aid your recovery,' she said, sitting on the edge of his bed and handing him a glass and a bottle. I keep these for medicinal purposes.'

'Most considerate.'

'"Do unto others as you'd have them do unto you".'

'A sound motto.' They filled their glasses. 'Cheers!'

'Bottoms up, Richard!' They drank. 'How was it?'

'Delicious.'

'It was drink what killed my late husband, you know,' she said, sipping from her glass. 'He was a fool. Went over to see some friend of his from the Navy in Birkenhead and got so drunk that he fell off the ferry coming back. Drowned.' She snorted. 'And this was a man who'd been at Dunkirk. God rest his soul, the daft bastard!' She moved closer to the invalid. 'I miss him, Dick. Painfully.'

'Of course . . . '

'But I mustn't burden you with my problems.' She looked at him shrewdly. 'Are you married, by the way?'

'No,' he said. 'Well, I was – briefly.'

'What happened?'

'It didn't work out.'

'I'm sorry. Got a girlfriend at the moment?'

'No, not right now.'

'Well, don't let life pass you by, love.'

She drank deep and gave him a long, lingering smile.

Dick realized that he was cornered and looked for escape.

'I won't.' He twitched about. 'Oh . . . dear me!'

'What's the matter?'

'I'm itching like crazy.' He tried to get rid of her. 'I take it you've had chicken pox, Mrs O'Callaghan.'

'Maureen,' she said, confidingly. 'Oh, yes, I've had the lot in my time. Where does it irritate you, sweetheart?'

'Oh. All over.'

'Like me to rub something on?' she volunteered.

'No, you mustn't, really.'

'It'd be a pleasure to give you some relief.'

Dick spluttered. 'I need to go to the toilet.'

'There's a jerry under the bed. Shall I hand it up?'

He held his stomach. 'I feel sick!'

'Oh, no. I hope it wasn't that stout . . . '

The sketch was an uproarious success. Morton Stanley was dressed as a doctor, Ian Deasey was the legless man in the wheelchair and Hedda Kennedy was a stylish nurse. Moira stood in the wings and watched the way that her husband took every opportunity to touch Hedda. He never missed a laugh.

'Now, it was the left leg, wasn't it?' he asked.

'That's right,' said Ian. 'Left.'

'See how easily these errors are made?'

'How do you mean, Doctor?'

'A simple case of mistaken truncation.'

'I don't understand.'

'We took off the wrong pin, mate. Sorry.'

Ian waited for the gales of laughter to subside.

'What?'

'But we've done the right one as well,' said the doctor, cheerfully. 'At no extra charge.' Hoots of delight. The nurse whispered into the doctor's ear and he passed on the good news. 'Every cloud has a silver lining, Mr Jenkins.'

'How's that, Doctor?'

'Bloke in Ward Seven wants to buy your slippers.'

Thunderous applause came. It was ironic. With only one leg, Ian had been unable to raise a titter. With none at all, he got a laugh a line. He and Hedda were delighted as they came off-stage but Morton Stanley's grin turned sour.

'What a mess! What a bloody shambles!'

'But they loved it!' said Ian.

'Ha! Liverpool! They'd laugh if you strangled a cat and ate it. What are we going to look like in London?' He rounded on Hedda. 'Deasey has some idea of timimg but you were dire, dearie. Rehearsal tomorrow. Ten o'clock in your dressing room. I'll spare your blushes in front of the whole company. We need to work at this . . . '

He stalked off grandly and left them speechless.

Edith had come to her daughter's house for tea and was helping to peel the potatoes in the kitchen. She had been told about the offer of the job at the doctor's surgery.

'I don't know why you're hesitating,' she said. 'Your husband buggered off when it suited him.'

Janet shook her head. 'It's not that, Mum. Think of the hours. I'd be working till seven most nights. What about Alan?'

'He can come to me. He seems to like my shop well enough, the little imp.' She cackled. 'No guessing where he gets that from!'

'Probably his grandmother,' said Janet, shooting her an old-fashioned look. Edith chortled. 'Why are you so keen that I should take this job, anyway?'

'Because I think you have to look after yourself. That's what you learned in the war, wasn't it?'

'The war's over, Mum. Things've changed.'

'Men haven't.'

There was a long pause as Janet weighed it all up.

'What will Annabel think?' she said.

'Does Annabel think?' Edith sneered. 'Take the job.'

Ian Deasey had spent a troubled night in the same room as Hedda. A curtain still separated their single beds but there was no Dick Dobson to act as chaperone. Instead of sleeping heavily, Ian lay awake and listened to the breathing of the gorgeous woman in a silk nightdress who was only feet away from him. It was frustrating.

Next morning, he called on the patient. Dick was low.

'Can I get you anything?' offered Ian.

'No, thanks,' said Dick, wearily. 'I have Mrs O'Callaghan and the *Liverpool Echo*, with Scott and Hodges on the wireless doing our material. What more can a man desire?' He sighed and lay back in his bed. 'Where's Hedda?'

'Rehearsing with Morton Stanley.'

'All go, isn't it? Stanley and Hedda. You and Hedda. A roaring success.' Dick was bitter. 'It makes me feel spotty, redundant and excluded.'

'You'll soon be better,' Ian assured. 'Then you, me and Hedda will team up again. We're going all the way.'

'All the way where?'

'Well . . . all the way . . . to there.'

'I can always tell when you're lying, Deasey,' said Dick. 'Your left eye wanders.'

Morton Stanley locked the door of the dressing room so that he could rehearse in private with Hedda Kennedy. He went through the section where he took the clipboard from his nurse to study the case-notes of his patient.

'What we could try,' he said, 'as an experiment, is this. I swing round, keeping my eyes on Deasey, and instead of taking the clipboard, I do this.' He grabbed her breast and she promptly jumped away. 'Well? It'd get a laugh.'

'I'm sure it would.'

'Shall we try it again?'

'I think I get the general drift.'

He stopped circling her with a predatory eye and became the Grand Old Man of the theatre, dispensing wise counsel.

'You know, Hedda,' he said. 'Deasey and Dobson, they're the eternal foot-soldiers, the spear-carriers of the comic stage, I'm afraid. You – you're raw, you need a lot of hard work, but you've got something . . . Star quality!' He moved in on her. 'I've had a good living and a lot of joy out of the theatre. I'd like to put a little bit back in, Hedda. I'd like to make you a star.'

Before she could stop him, he kissed and groped her but she made a quick recovery. His eyes popped out as she brought a knee up into his crotch. He doubled in pain.

'You're a dirty old man!'

'You little cow!

Moira Stanley let herself in with the pass key and saw a scene that had been played out by her husband many times.

'She threw herself at me,' he bleated.

'And you just happened to be there to catch her!' Her

bilious eye hit Hedda. 'As for you, you little minx . . . '

When Ian Deasey and Hedda Kennedy came out on-stage that night, the sketch had undergone a transmutation. Morton Stanley got just as many laughs but with a very different script. They were bemused extras for most of the time.

'May I see the notes, Nurse?' said Stanley, taking the clipboard from her and looking at the case-notes. 'Oh, very nasty. A tragic miscalculation.'

'How do you mean?' said Ian.

'You won't be able to do it any more.'

There was a huge laugh. Ian was completely thrown.

'Do what?' he said, utterly confused.

'The necessary!'

Morton Stanley delivered the line out front and mugged at the audience to get the message home. They shook with mirth. The nurse came across to whisper something in his ear and another line was altered to great effect.

'Too late for that, love,' said Stanley. 'I'm afraid that you missed your chance . . . '

There was a double-meaning in the line that made Hedda smart but all she could do was to stand there while her boss got the laughs at her expense. The doctor bent over the patient with a leer.

'We could try a splint, I suppose.'

Ian was lost. 'But . . . '

'Never mind, old son. Every cloud has a silver lining.'

'Does it?'

'Well . . . ' Stanley milked the pause. 'You'll sleep better.'

They took their bow to great acclaim then came into the wings as the dancing girls went bouncing on. Ian and Hedda were deeply hurt the way they had been misled and exploited. Morton Stanley had made complete stooges of them.

'You changed it all!' accused Ian. 'I didn't know what I was supposed to do.'

'Improvise,' said Morton Stanley, spreading his palms. 'If you can't improvise, you're sunk.

'What?'

'But then you're sunk anyway.'

'Why?' asked Ian.

'You're fired,' said Moira, coldly. 'Both of you.'

'What did we do?'

'Ask your girlfriend.'

'Hedda . . . ?'

Ian turned to her and she shook her head miserably. Pious and unconcerned, Stanley stood behind his indomitable wife and let her do the dirty work.

'Conduct prejudicial to company discipline,' said Moira.

'He tried to get in my knickers,' said Hedda.

'Monstrous accusation!' snorted Stanley.

Ian stared in dismay at his fallen hero. Taking a hip flask from his back pocket, Morton Stanley took a swig before strolling past them and going back on-stage to another burst of rapturous applause. Ian turned to Moira.

'What about the final curtain call?'

'You've just had it.'

There was no point in lingering. Their brief success had been snuffed out before it had come to anything. There was no justice. Ian Deasey and Hedda Kennedy got out of their costumes and wiped off their make-up before gathering up their things. He took a wistful look around a place which had held so much promise for him, while all she remembered was her encounter there with the slobbering Morton Stanley.

Something else now worried them. How were they going to break the terrible news to Dick? His hopes had been riding on the Liverpool Theatre Royal just as much as theirs. If they had made their mark there, they would have toured the country with Morton Stanley for months. Dick would have to be told. After the chicken pox, the sexual assault from Mrs O'Callaghan and the galling fact that Scott and Hodges were in employment and using their material, it would be a crippling blow.

As they walked out, they could hear the riotous applause above them as Morton Stanley took the audience through Dear Old Donegal'. They could not bear to listen and hurried out through the stage door and into the alley beyond. On a cold night in a cheerless city, they were two orphans flung out into the storm.

'What are we going to do?' said Ian, sadly

'We'll find something.'

'Fat chance of that, Hedda.'

'You wait.'

'I did wait. For years. And this is how it turned out.'

'We had bad luck, that's all.'

'I'm jinxed,' he moaned. 'I'm a doomed man.'

'Don't be silly.

'I've got no job, no act, no partner, no money.' His hands gestured hopelessly. 'Nothing.'

Hedda stepped in close to him.

'You've got me,' she said.

She wrapped her arms around him. Taken aback at first, he responded with increasing urgency and they were soon locked in a passionate embrace.

'Ian . . . ' Dick coughed loudly. 'Ian!'

The couple eventually parted and turned to see Dick Dobson standing there with a bandaged face and in great embarrassment. Beside him was the last person in the world whom Ian wanted to meet at that moment.

'Hello, Ian,' she said, quietly.

Janet had come to find her husband.

CHAPTER 11

Dressed like the local squire, Rudi Lorimer strolled proudly through the meadow with Dick Dobson at his shoulder. The naval base had long been deserted and it was now no more than a collection of dilapidated huts in the long grass. An air of decay hung over the whole place. As they walked past what had once been an office, there was a loud moo and a cow ambled out with wide-eyed curiosity. Dick was revolted by the scene around him, but Lorimer was patently inspired.

'A magnificent site, isn't it!'

'Not exactly the Taj Mahal.'

'The setting, you nitwit. The lay-out. It's perfect.'

Dick was mystified. 'Is it?'

'Made to measure.'

'Only an undertaker would measure this dump.' He shrugged an apology. 'Sorry. I've seen too many of these sorts of places in my time. I guess I'm prejudiced.'

'That's the difference between us, Dick,' said Lorimer with condescension. 'You see what was yesterday, and I see what might be tomorrow. You lack vision.'

'Do I?'

'Never judge anything on face value. Always try to see the hidden potential. That's the secret of success.' He strode boldly forward through the grass. 'The leap of faith.'

'Careful!' said Dick.

'Being one step ahead,' said Lorimer, putting a foot straight into a cow pat. 'Agh! Damn!'

'Pooh.'

'You idiot, Dobson!'

'*I* didn't do it.'

'Why didn't you warn me, man?'

'You were one step ahead.'

Lorimer tried to clean his expensive brogue in the long grass and Dick grinned at his companion's lack of vision.

'Give me your handkerchief!' demanded Lorimer.

Somewhere among the huts, a cow was laughing.

Janet Deasey was enjoying the job at the doctor's surgery. It kept her busy and was full of visual interest. As she cleared the papers from Jeremy Pollock's desk, he held an X-Ray up to the light to examine it.

'They take a rattling good snap down at St John's, don't they?' he said. 'Have a dekko.'

'Very good,' she agreed. 'Rather flattering.'

'Oh, yes? Who is it, then? Eh?'

'Mr Reynolds. Strangulated hernia.'

Pollock goggled. 'How in God's name can you tell that?'

'It's written on page two of his file.'

'Bravo!' he said, laughing. 'Feminine intuition.'

'Anything else you need to know, Jeremy,' she said with a smile, 'don't be afraid to ask.'

'Well, as a matter of fact, there is something.'

'Yes?'

'I've been invited to attend the BMA dinner on Thursday night. Quite a grand affair, I'm told, and old Wakeley's in the chair. How would you like to come?' He saw her hesitation. 'You're part of the team, after all.'

'Well, that's very generous of you.'

'It's a small reward for all your labours, Janet.'

'What about Annabel?'

'Oh, she'll be there,' said Pollock, airily. 'Never one to turn down free grub. We'll go as a foursome.'

'Ah, so I'm partnering old Wakeley, am I?'

'Will your husband mind?'

'His hard luck if he does!' said Janet. 'Thank you.'

Bedtime at Walthamstow was no longer the joyous event it had been on his demob. Ian Deasey was still in the doghouse. He lay beside his wife that night and tried to point out the consolations of his brief foray into show business.

'I earned a few bob in Liverpool,' he argued.

'Until you got the boot. It was supposed to be a two-month engagement and it lasted two minutes.'

'There's still some money to come from the army.'

'When?'

'I don't know. Soon.'

'And what are we going to live on in the meantime?'

'I'm doing my best, Janet,' he said. 'Give me a chance. All I need is an opening. Just one decent push and I'd be right up there.' Ominous silence. 'You listening to me?'

'No, love,' she said with a yawn. 'It's not because I'm not interested, but I'm tired. I have to get Alan off to school in the morning, go to the surgery, come home to give him his lunch, go back to the surgery then make tea for both of you in the evening. It's a treadmill.'

'I could have a go at some cooking,' offered Ian.

'Things are bad enough as it is.'

'Janet!'

'Save your strength for the big push.' He snuggled up to her. 'Only not tonight.' She switched off the light.

'You've never seen me perform, have you?'

'With your little blonde friend? Nearly. I didn't actually witness the event, as it were . . . '

'Don't start that again,' he said. 'My relationship with Hedda Kennedy is strictly professional.'

'You mean, she *charges*?'

'Of course not!'

'Calm down, calm down,' she said. 'I can't take any more of your artistic temperament tonight. I need my sleep.'

She nodded straight off and Ian fumed in the darkness.

Dick Dobson bounded up to the front door of the prefab and knocked. It was opened by a flour-bespattered figure in an apron. Ian Deasey was learning to cook. Dick raised his hat.

'Good afternoon, madam,' he said. 'Is your husband in?'

'What do you want?' growled Ian.

'Nice to see you, too, old chum. Going to ask me in?'

Dick stepped into the house and closed the door after him. A loud hissing noise told Ian that something was boiling over and he raced off to the kitchenette. When Dick joined him, the chef was lifting a pan off the hob and almost scalding himself. The whole place was littered with cooking utensils and covered in white flour.

'Good to see you keeping so busy, Deasey.'

'I'm fine, thank you,' said Ian.'

'Rudi sends his regards, by the way.'

'Lorimer's a crook. Should be locked up.'

'We'll come to him in a moment . . . How's Hedda?'

'She's teaching me how to play the ukelele.'

'What about work?'

'We've got a booking,' lied Ian. 'Several, in fact.'

'Good show!'

'Everything's going perfectly.'

'Then you're managing without me?'

'Yes.'

'So you wouldn't be interested in joining us at Burwood for a few days?'

'No. What for?'

'Rudi's got a rather exciting little scheme going.'

'You never learn, do you!'

'Give the man credit, Ian,' said Dick. 'He works bloody hard and he's been damn good to me – and you. He's converting an old naval base into a holiday camp. Thousands of happy families with thousands of pounds to spend.'

'You're joking!'

'No, I'm not.'

'What does he want me to do – head the escape committee?'

'Rudi's not very happy with his builders.'

'They can't be any benter than he is.

'Bearing in mind your years of experience with Walthamstow Council, I suggested that you might be able to pop down and give him the benefit of your expertise. Take a look at the work in progress.'

Ian shook his head. 'I don't think so, Dick.'

'There'd be a small fee, I'm sure.

'You mean, you're sure the fee would be small.'

'What are you earning at present?'

'I'm doing all right, mate,' said Ian, defensively. 'I've got a nice little act going with Hedda.' He stuck in the knife. 'Now, you wouldn't want me to go letting my partner down, would you?'

Cooper's Corsetry reverberated to grunts and groans as Janet Deasey helped her mother to shift a heavy display cabinet.

When they had moved it a few feet, they paused for a rest.

'Take a breather!' said Edith, puffing. 'As for this BMA thing, why shouldn't you go? Spoil yourself for a change. You deserve a little treat, Janet.'

'After moving this, I deserve a medal.'

'I don't know how you put up with it.'

'What?'

'Ian. His whims. His ways.'

'Do I have any choice, Mum?'

'Of course you do,' said Edith, tartly. 'Same choice as he's got. Get yourself a fancy man. That'd shake him up.'

Janet was shocked. 'That's hardly the sort of advice you expect to hear from a mother.'

'I'm talking to you as a woman. You've got to look out for yourself, girl. Don't let the daft sod shove you around.'

'I don't.'

'Yes, you do. One word from you and he does what he likes. Give him a taste of his own medicine.'

'Is this the voice of experience I'm hearing?'

'It's the voice of a loving mother!' said Edith as she grabbed the cabinet again. 'Let's get this bugger shifted.'

'Where to?'

'Towards me. Give it a good push.'

Janet shoved with all her might and the cabinet tilted over like the leaning tower of Pisa. Edith yelled, Janet let go and the cabinet thudded back down again. There was a casualty. Janet was writhing in pain.

'My back!' she moaned. 'I've put my back out.'

'I knew I should have waited for help.'

'Who from?'

'Never mind,' said Edith, dismissively. 'Sit down, love. You look terrible.' She lowered her daughter towards the chair but it only produced louder groans. 'We'd better get you home. I can move that bloody cabinet later.'

'On your own?'

Edith ignored the question and slipped an arm around Janet's waist. Letting themselves out of the shop, they returned gingerly to the prefab. In the kitchenette, Alan was facing another kind of agony. His father had cooked him savoury dumplings for tea. They lay on the plate like molten cricket balls, garnished with liquid horse manure.

'I can't eat that vomit, Dad!' protested the boy.

'OK,' said Ian, accepting defeat. 'Off to the chip shop. Here's some money.' He saw Janet hobbling in on her mother's arm and went over in concern. 'What happened?'

'She hurt her back,' said Edith. 'Doing a man's job.'

Marshall Gould poured the sherry out and handed Ian Deasey a glass of Consolation Cream. His client sipped it gratefully. Being in the agent's plush office again gave Ian a sharp twinge. Unemployment was demeaning.

'I saw two old chums of yours the other day,' said Gould. 'Lieutenants Scott and Hodges. Tommy and Jerry.'

'And what are they up to?'

'Oh, just bits and pieces. Times are hard, Ian. There's not an awful lot about – as I'm sure you've noticed.'

'We'd settle for a bit or a piece, Mr Gould.'

'Is your partner back in town, then?'

'Dick? No,' said Ian. 'I'm working with someone else.'

'Who's that, then?'

'She's called Hedda Kennedy.'

The agent was unhappy. '*She*?'

'That's right.'

'No relation to old Paddy Kennedy, is she? The Comical Kerry Man. He was good.' Ian shook his head. 'He's dead now, anyway. Most of the real comedians are.'

'Hedda's a very pretty girl,' said Ian.

'That's always a good start. Plays the piano, does she?'

'No, but she can play the ukelele.'

'*Anyone* can play the ukelele,' said Gould with scorn.

'I can't.'

'Ian.' The agent lowered his voice to pass on a trade secret. 'I have to tell you. I've never found women particularly funny. You may disagree, of course . . . '

Ian sagged. 'I know what you're saying.'

The annual dinner of the British Medical Association was held in the banqueting room of a smart West End hotel. Men wore black ties and the ladies were decked out in ballgowns and cocktail dresses. A band played light music in the background while the assembled medics worked their way through a three-course meal and compared notes about general practice.

Janet Deasey sat at the top table with Annabel, Jeremy Pollock and Dr Wakeley, the old and sententious president of the BMA. Janet felt slightly guilty that she had not told Ian where she was going, but she reasoned that – since he himself was out somewhere – he need never know where she had been. The giggling Annabel was having a wonderful time as she hung on to Pollock's every word, though he was far more interested in Janet than in his nominal partner.

Wakeley nodded to the bandleader. Music ceased and a hush fell on the room. He rose majestically to his feet.

'Ladies and gentlemen . . . the loyal toast.'

There was a general scraping of chairs as everyone got up.

'His Majesty the King!' said Wakeley, patriotically.

'His Majesty the King!' chorused the guests.

Glasses were raised, then seats were resumed. Amused by the solemnity, Janet pulled a face at Annabel who screeched with girlish laughter. Hundreds of matches and lighters flared up as almost everyone in the room began smoking. Wakeley himself puffed on a cigar of Churchillian proportions.

'You'll regret it, Jeremy,' he warned. 'Should exercise your lungs, you know. Smoking is good for you.'

Pollock ignored him and leaned across to Janet.

'Glad you came?' he whispered.

'Very glad.'

'Ian didn't mind?' She shook her head. 'Good . . . '

Ian Deasey was more concerned about his grass skirt than the whereabouts of his wife. He and Hedda were walking along a corridor in the hotel, dressed as Hawaiian maids with roses in their hair. Ian had shirt, black tie and dinner jacket on the upper half of his body, but Hedda was virtually naked.

A passing waiter stopped to gape at her.

'Is there a place we can sit?' she asked.

'What about my lap?' the waiter leered.

'I'd prefer somewhere clean.'

The dancing girls headed for the rear of the stage.

'Officers of the association, gentlemen, and – for the first time in our history – ladies . . . ' Dr Wakeley was making his speech in a soporific monotone. 'This is, for me, both a glad and a sad occasion. Glad, that after seven years of absence during the long conflict, I can once again welcome you all to this annual rendezvous. And sad, because it is the last occasion on which I have the honour to address you as your president . . . '

Warm applause rippled. Wakeley inhaled his cigar. A feeling of goodwill prevailed. He went on to kill it.

'Indeed, doubly sad,' he continued, 'because, as I depart, I see changes being imposed on our profession from on high. Changes which threaten to undermine the very spirit and fabric of our calling . . . '

'What's he talking about?' asked Annabel.

'The National Health Service,' explained Janet.

'Why doesn't he say so?'

'He just did.'

In convoluted language, Dr Wakeley went on to prophesy doom for the medical profession if the Labour Government went ahead with its plans. Shouts of agreement were mixed with calls of protest. The general view was that an annual dinner should be an occasion to enjoy and not a forum for political debate.

Wakeley continued to plough his deep and tiresome furrow.

Waiting on stage behind the curtains, Ian and Hedda could not hear the speech in detail but the surge of complaint reached them. He wondered what new ordeal now awaited them.

'Who are these lot?' he asked.

'Freemasons, I think.'

They looked at each other in a moment of existential despair.

'What are we doing here, Hedda?'

'It's work, isn't it?'

'Is it?' He looked down at knobbly knees beneath his grass skirt. 'Is this the way for a grown man to carry on?'

'You should have thought about that earlier.'

'I did,' he told her. 'I did. It's just that I always imagined something a bit more . . . I don't know . . . dignified?'

'Long black limousines? Supper at the Savoy?'

'It doesn't have to be a Royal Command Performance. Just something with a bit more dignity.' He shook his skirt. 'Look at this lot. There's things moving in there.'

'Where?' She explored his grass. 'Let me see.'

'Keep your hands to yourself!' he said, rustling out of her reach. 'Have you no shame, girl!'

Muted applause signalled the end of the speech and they took up their positions. Dr Wakeley announced them and the curtains parted. They were on. With Hedda strumming a ukelele, they did a suggestive hula-hula dance as Ian sang.

'She's my little Hawaiian lass
All she's got is a skirt of grass.
I know it's not much to cover her . . .'

Hedda wiggled her hips and joined in the chorus.

'Hula-hula, wacki-wacki, nicky-nacky noo!'

Janet Deasey was crimson with embarrassment. She was ready to die. Annabel compounded her misery by telling everyone that the male Hula-Hula girl was Janet's husband. As the act went into a second excruciating verse, Janet could stick it no longer. Leaping to her feet to leave, however, she hurt her back and let out a scream of pain.

'Is there a doctor in the house?' yelled out a wag.

The burst of laughter completely threw Ian. He gaped in amazement as his wife was helped out by Pollock. Ian ran out after them with swishing urgency and Hedda danced gamely on like the boy on the burning deck.

Ian caught them up at the car but Janet refused to speak to a man in a grass skirt. Pollock drove her off.

The row began with a slammed door and moved to the bedroom.

'I've had enough, Ian,' she said, lowering herself carefully on to the bed. 'That's the last straw!'

'Janet, please,' he soothed. 'Don't be so angry.'

'How do you think I felt? In front of all those people? My husband up on that stage!'

'I didn't know you'd be there. It was one of those things. An accident. It can't be helped.'

'Can't be helped? What – prancing around like a fairy! I'm sick of you. Sick of all your nonsense. Sick and tired and fed up to the back-teeth.'

'So what do you want me to do?'

'Sod off!'

'Janet!'

'Go back to the rotten desert! Go back to Dick – and take your tart in a grass skirt with you!'

'She's not my tart!'

Janet grabbed the alarm clock and threw it at him. Ian ducked and it hit the Monarch of the Glen between the antlers.

'Just go!' she screamed. 'Leave me alone! You're hopeless. You're completely hopeless.'

'Right, then! If that's what you bloody think!' Ian ran out into the road and slammed the front door after him. He bent down to yell back through the letterbox. 'I can earn proper money! I've had jobs offered. Proper jobs. Janet . . . ?'

But the prefab was silent and unyielding.

Alone in the dark of his bedroom, Alan Deasey bit his lip. He had overheard every savage word of the exchange between his parents and was powerless to do anything about it.

Ian's motorbike started up with a vengeance.

'Dad!' he called.

CHAPTER 12

Burwood House was a stately pile set in acres of rolling parkland, a symbol of aristocratic power and a monument to exquisite taste. Rudi Lorimer emerged from the house in his country clobber with Dick Dobson trotting at his heels like a springer spaniel. A man of taste with a love of power, Lorimer had bought himself a house which reflected his personality. The gleaming Bentley which stood on the forecourt was the final touch.

Dick played the faithful retainer to a fault. He ran forward to open the rear door of the car so that his employer could climb in. But the vehicle was already occupied.

'Dear God!' shouted Lorimer, recoiling in fear.

Ian Deasey's head surfaced from the back seat. He gave a yawn worthy of the MGM lion then mumbled his apologies.

'Sorry about this, Mr Lorimer,' he said. 'Ran out of petrol, I'm afraid.'

'What the hell are you doing here?' said Dick.

'I've thought over your offer.'

'What offer?' said Lorimer, peevishly.

'Dick said you needed advice. On your new project.'

'You told me you weren't interested,' said Dick.

'Only because you caught me at a bad moment.'

'Ha!' grunted Lorimer. 'Your whole life is a succession of bad moments, isn't it, Deasey?'

'It seems that way sometimes,' conceded Ian. He looked from one to the other. 'Any chance of a bit of breakfast?'

'Later, maybe,' said Lorimer. 'If I think you deserve it.'

Alan Deasey sat at the table in the kitchenette and pushed lumpy porridge around with his spoon. Janet was frenziedly cleaning everything in sight just to remain occupied.

'Are you feeling better?' he asked.

'I'll survive, thank you.'

'Where's Dad gone?'

'I don't know, I'm afraid.'

'When's he coming back?'

'I don't know that either,' she confessed. 'He didn't say. Now eat your porridge and stop worrying.'

Alan was adamant. 'I want to know where Dad is.'

'I haven't a clue where he is because he didn't see fit to tell me – or you, for that matter.'

'I was in bed.'

'You obviously weren't asleep.'

'How could I sleep with that noise going on?' He looked up at her. 'You told him to sod off.'

'Yes, and I meant it. So there!'

'Has he run off with another woman?'

'What other woman would have him?' she snapped.

Alan brightened. 'You're still friends, then?'

Janet stopped dusting and came sadly over to him.

'He's still my husband and he's still your dad.'

'What's going to happen now?'

'That's up to your father,' she said with a sigh. 'For the time being, we're just going to carry on as normal. Just like we did before he came home.'

'Oh.'

Alan stared down morosely at his breakfast.

The Bentley crested a hill with majestic ease then swept down towards the camp. Dick brought it to a halt outside the gate. Above their heads, the name of the base was painted in fading letters – HMS *Amazon.* It was an apt title for a site which had now been turned into a river of mud on which dirty Nissen huts floated like crocodiles waiting for their prey. There was little activity. Harrup, the site foreman, came bustling over with a roll of plans under his arm. He was a flat-faced man with a know-it-all manner. He tugged a dutiful forelock for Lorimer but regarded the immaculate Dick and the unshaven Ian with misgiving.

Rudi Lorimer flicked a hand at his passenger.

'This is Ian Deasey,' he introduced. 'A friend of young Richard's. Down here for a few days in the fresh air.'

'How d'you do?' grunted Harrup.

'Nice day for it,' said Ian.

'I hear you've run into problems, Harrup.'

'Yes, Mr Lorimer,' said the foreman, seriously. 'You have to remember that these places were slung up in a couple of weeks to house a lot of squaddies. They weren't built for comfort and they weren't built to last . . . Latrine blocks with a soakaway.' He wrinkled his nose. 'Just a glorified cesspit, to be honest.'

'Could we see the plans, please?' said Lorimer.

'Of course,' said the other, unfurling the first sheet. 'Look, sir. Here are your blocks. There's nothing linked at all to any of the accommodation.'

'Deasey.' Lorimer motioned him in to view the plan.

'You know about drainage, do you?' said Harrup, worried.

'It's just a hobby with him,' said Dick.

Ian perused the plan with care then viewed the site.

'Well,' he said, 'I'm only an amateur, you understand, but I think we should take a look over there . . . '

He led the way purposefully between the huts with the others at his heels. Ian guided them fifty yards then stopped.

'Right here,' he said, referring to the plan. 'Between huts eight and nine. Access three. Steel cover.'

'Forgive me, Mr Lorimer,' interrupted Harrup, 'but this is ridiculous. There is no main drainage channel out here. Just a rather crude soakaway arrangement.'

'A cesspit, you called it,' observed Lorimer. 'If Deasey is pulling my leg, you can throw him into the pit.'

Ian found the manhole cover and chuckled in triumph.

'That's our baby. Number three. This is where your number ones meet your number twos. Providing you haven't got a blockage anywhere.'

'This is a storm drain,' argued Harrup. 'It's just a rainwater conduit.'

Lorimer was not convinced. 'May we *see*, Mr Harrup?'

'What – lift it up?'

'Won't take a second,' said Ian. 'Come on.'

Ian, Harrup and a reluctant Dick strained to lift the steel cover. Lorimer peered into the chamber and clutched at his throat. The stench was overpowering.

'Dear God!' he yelled.

'The fleet's in!' said Ian, looking down the chamber. 'What did I tell you? Yes, you've got a lovely clear passage down there, Mr Lorimer. No drainage problems at all.'

'Shut it – for heaven's sake!' ordered Lorimer.

The lid clanged down and a nervous Harrup wiped his eyes on his coat. He had been trying to fleece his boss.

'Mr Harrup,' said Lorimer, coldly. 'I won't be requiring your services any longer and I don't expect a bill. Understood?'

The site foreman shot a look of venom at Ian and slunk away. Dick was on the point of throwing up but the stink of raw sewage had merely whetted Ian's appetite. He grinned.

'Have I earned that breakfast now?'

Janet Deasey lay face down on the examination table in the consulting room while Jeremy Pollock gently massaged her neck and back. The events of the night before weighed on them.

'Quite a performance,' he said, 'one way and another.'

'What did Dr Wakeley say about it all?'

'He took it remarkably well, Janet. He feels that it rather took people's attention off that awful speech of his about the Health Service.'

'I could've killed Ian!' she asserted.

'Yes,' said Pollock, amiably. 'I doubt if a jury would have convicted you for it. What they call justifiable homicide.' His fingers found a tender spot and she winced. 'That's it. Touch of fibrositis. Been sleeping in a draught?'

'I thought it was just a bit of a strain.'

'It's a little more than that,' he said. 'Be careful you don't make any sudden moves for the time being. Until things settle.'

'I'll bear that in mind, Doctor.'

The door opened abruptly and Wakeley bumbled in. Pollock jumped back guiltily and Janet adjusted her dress.

'Sorry,' said Wakeley, hiding his shock. 'I didn't know that you were in here.'

'Janet's got a touch of fibrositis, it appears.'

'I see.' Wakeley's disapproval was obvious. 'Well, you want to be more careful.'

Now standing up again, Janet nodded in agreement.

'That's just what Jeremy was saying . . . '

☆ ☆ ☆

The study at Burwood House was a huge, oak-panelled room. Lorimer and Ian Deasey stood behind the massive desk and pored over the drawings relating to the conversion. The project was called Happylands but it made Ian deeply unhappy.

'To be frank, Mr Lorimer,' he said, 'I'd rather hoped not to be doing this sort of thing again.'

'Doing what?'

'Toilets.'

'Come on, man,' encouraged the other. 'This is a big project. Big profits. I'm offering you part of it.'

'But it's not the part I really want.'

'You're just like Dobbo, aren't you? Can't see the wood for the trees. Think of all those people, Ian.'

'All those toilets.'

'All that money!' said Lorimer. 'Families, getting away for a couple of weeks for the first time since the war. Money to burn. After a good time. Damn the expense!'

'They won't think twice about spending a penny, then?'

'They'll spend a fortune. And all of it here – on site. Bars, restaurants, entertainment, all laid on. Dance bands, top acts . . . '

'What about me and Dick?'

'I'm cutting the pair of you in.'

'I meant – as performers.'

'Performers?'

'Why not?'

'Ian,' said Lorimer, candidly, 'this isn't going to be like the old days. These are families, middle-class types. We can't have any barrack-room stuff.'

'I'm not stupid, Rudi.'

'I know you're not.'

'So.' Ian looked him in the eye. 'If I sort out the lavs, Dick and I will want a spot on the old variety bill. Is that a deal?'

'A deal?' Lorimer smiled. 'You're learning, Ian.'

'Well . . . ?'

As Lorimer pondered, Dick brought in a tray of coffee.

'Fair enough,' decided Lorimer. 'It's a deal.'

'What is?' asked Dick.

'Just put it down there, my good man,' ordered Ian.

'Certainly, m'lady,' returned Dick.

'We were just discussing the entertainment provision for Happylands,' explained Lorimer.

'Oh,' said Dick. 'Deasey hasn't suggested us doing our old act for the happy campers, has he?'

'No, he hasn't. We won't lift the manhole cover on that particular drain.'

'I'm talking about a new act,' said Ian. 'You and me.'

Dick was intrigued. 'I see . . . '

Edith Cooper was in the fitting room at her shop, helping her daughter to try on a new corset. Janet was not at all sure that she needed a foundation garment, even if it did come with a generous discount. Her mother finished doing it up for her.

'There you are, then,' said Edith. 'How's that?'

'Feels a bit tight, Mum.'

'It'll give that bad back of yours some support, Janet. And do wonders for the old posture.'

'If you say so.'

'I do. And I say this, too . . . You did the right thing.'

Janet pursed her lips. 'I hope so.'

'Mark my words,' said her mother. 'Once he's missed a couple of hot dinners, he'll soon come crawling back with his tail between his legs. They're all the same.'

'Ian isn't.'

Edith was scathing. 'Men are only good for one thing and they're usually not much cop at that, if truth be told.' The shop bell tinkled and her professional voice rang out. 'I'll be with you in just a moment.'

'No hurry, love,' said a man's voice, familiarly.

Janet reacted with surprise and looked at her mother. Edith forced a smile and went bustling into the shop to the waiting figure of Frank Parsons. The Borough Engineer was lounging against the counter with a beatific grin.

'Can I help you?' said Edith with great formality.

'I got you some kidneys . . . '

Parsons put a package on the counter then turned pale as Janet stepped out of the fitting room.

'Hello, Mrs Deasey . . . '

'Mr Parsons . . . '

'How's Ian?' he asked.

'He's fine, thanks.' She smiled thinly. 'How's Rose?'

'Very well. The wife is . . . very well.' He coughed and sidled to the door. 'Well, I'll be off. I hope you enjoy the kidneys, Mrs Cooper.' He opened the door. 'Cheerio, then.'

'Thank you, Frank.'

The door shut behind him and Edith did not flinch beneath her daughter's quizzical gaze. She picked up the kidneys and sniffed them.

'He's a very generous man is Mr Parsons,' she said.

'He wasn't very generous with Ian.'

'No, well . . . '

Thorpe's Farm was a short drive from Burwood House and the two establishments were already co-operating effectively with each other. As the Bentley stood in the farmyard, a couple of yokels loaded dairy produce of all kinds into the boot. Dick Dobson leaned nonchalantly against the wing of the car with a cigarette. Ian was hypnotized.

'No shortages down here, then,' he said.

'I told you so,' reminded Dick. 'No shortages and no rationing. A land flowing with milk and honey. And all thanks to you-know-who.'

'All right, mate. Don't rub it in.'

'I won't, Ian.' Dick doused his cigarette. 'Hey, are we really going to be doing the old routine?'

'Yes. Except that it'll have to be a new routine.'

'Sure you can deliver the goods?'

'You just watch me.'

Finishing their work, the yokels closed the boot of the car. Dick leaned into the rear seat and passed out two boxes of finest Scotch Whisky to them.

'There you go, my fine fellows,' he said. 'Convey my compliments to Squire Thorpe, would you? See you next week.'

'Can I drive?' begged Ian.

'Only if you're very careful,' warned Dick. 'Last time you drove a car of Rudi's, it never lived to tell the tale.'

Ian promised to drive with great caution and they set off. The sheer luxury of the Bentley exhilarated him.

'This is the life, Dick. I must have one of these.'

'Wouldn't you miss the old bike?'

'Don't talk about my wife like that!' They laughed but Ian

was immediately contrite. 'No, I shouldn't either. You can't blame Janet. She's put up with a lot, one way and another.'

'Not any more, by the sound of it!'

'Don't say that.' Ian winced and changed the subject. 'Listen, we've got to get some labour in for this job. We'll need a few blokes who really know what they're doing.'

'Not like us, you mean?'

Ian was about to reply when a boy suddenly darted out of a hedgerow and ran right across their path. He was hunched up as if carrying something in the folds of his shirt. The car seemed certain to hit him. Braking hard, Ian swerved to avoid the lad and almost ended up in a ditch. Dick looked back to see the boy lying prostrate on the road.

'Oh, my God!' he exclaimed. 'You've killed him.'

Ian sprang from the car and rushed to the prone figure.

'Keep still, son' he advised, gently. 'Don't move . . . '

Janet Deasey was reading a magazine when she heard her son answer the door to admit Jeremy Pollock. She leapt up and tidied herself at once. He breezed in with a smile. Alan went back to his task of cleaning out the ashes from the grate.

'Hello, again,' he said, noting the general tidiness. 'You seem to have things well organized here, I must say.'

'Yes,' she said. 'Alan's helping me – for once.'

'That shows he's recovered from the chicken pox, then.' He beamed at her then remembered his excuse. 'Just been checking on a gallstone in the next road. Annabel's out pony-clubbing so . . . thought I'd pop in and see how things were. With your bad back.'

'That's very thoughtful of you,' she said. 'I'm fine and I'm being watched over by my guardian angel here.'

'Talking of which,' he said, lowering his voice, 'I got an earful from his nibs. "Unchaperoned attendance on a female patient." Wakeley's a real stickler for professional ethics.'

'I seem to be making trouble for everyone at the moment.'

'Don't feel guilty, Janet. It's not your fault.'

He gave her his most reassuring smile but she was looking over his shoulder. Pollock turned to see that Alan was watching them with a bucket of ashes in his hand. The conversation took a more neutral turn.

☆ ☆ ☆

The Bentley drew up in the middle of a small encampment. Carts, lorries and rusty old vans stood in a rough horseshoe on a patch of land at the side of the lane. Mangy horses grazed nearby. Smoke from a fire curled up into the sky. Ian and Dick got out of the car with the boy, who was covered all over in egg yolk and still slightly dazed. As a group of travellers formed around the newcomers, a tough-looking man in his thirties pushed forward. The boy was evidently his son.

'What happened?' he said in alarm.

'It's all right,' said Dick. 'No bones broken. Just the eggs.

'I'm sorry about that, guvnor,' said the man.

'We're just glad he wasn't hurt. He ran straight out in front of the motor. The boy is very lucky.'

'It won't happen again, I promise you. I'm his Dad. Eric Clayton's the name.' He turned to his son. 'I told you not to trespass, Walter! And if you've been stealing eggs off these gentlemen . . . '

Ian Deasey was looking around with fascination.

'What's all this, then?' he wondered.

'This lot? Struggling humanity,' said the man. 'We're homeless. Forced out on the road to survive.'

Dick felt sorry for them and for the boy. The boot was full of dairy produce and they could easily spare some.

'Now then, Walter,' he said, kindly. 'Fancy a dozen eggs to give to your Mum?'

'Got no Mum,' explained the father. 'Flying bomb. I was at Monte Cassino and the lad was in school.'

'I'm sorry,' said Dick. 'Which mob were you with?'

'Royal Engineers.'

'Get away! Deasey and I are ex-Royal Signals.'

The man was deferential. 'Officers, were you?'

'Almost. Deasey was an acting corporal.'

He got a tray of eggs out and the boy took him across to the old van in which he and his father lived.

'Royal Engineers, eh?'

'Full corporal,' said the man, proudly.'

'Do any construction work, by any chance?'

'Yes,' said the other. 'Plenty of it. Mainly fixing what the RAF had bombed. Roads, bridges, airfields . . . '

A slow smile spread across Ian's features.

'Busy at the moment, are you, Eric . . . ?'

CHAPTER 13

Alan Deasey was coming out of school at lunchtime with two friends when he saw his father. Ian was leaning casually against the wing of the Bentley. The children were greatly impressed.

'Dad!' Alan was delighted. 'What're you doing here?'

'Is that your car, Mr Deasey?' said Sam, a gaping boy.

'No,' said Ian, airily. 'I'm just using this until mine's delivered. I prefer a nice dark blue.'

'Can we have a ride?' begged Felicity, a giggling girl.

'Certainly.' Ian opened the rear door and they piled in. 'All aboard! But keep your feet off the seats.'

When the schoolchildren had been dropped off, the car drove to the Deasey prefab. Ian and Alan carried in boxes of dairy produce and put them in the kitchenette.

'You're not a spiv, are you, Dad?' said a worried Alan.

'What makes you think that?'

'You've got a big car.'

'So has the king.'

Alan looked at the food. 'What's Mum going to say?'

'Something complimentary for a change, I hope. Give her my love. Tell her there's plenty more where that came from.'

'Aren't you staying?'

'No,' said Ian, sadly. 'Don't worry. Few things to sort out first. Everything will turn out for the best, Alan. You just look after your mum for a bit.' He pressed a bundle of pound notes into the boy's hand. 'This will help.'

'Wow!'

Janet Deasey then appeared at the door. Her face was impassive as she looked at the provisions and the wad of notes. She asked Alan to leave them alone for a few minutes then confronted Ian across the cornucopia on the table.

'Where did this lot come from?' she demanded.

'From a farm. All right?'

'And the money?'

'Working. I've got a job.'

'Who with?'

'Lucky Lorimer.'

Her face crumpled. 'Oh, Ian!'

'No, listen,' he said, hurriedly, 'this is a real job. A proper job. It's a gentleman's agreement. Lorimer owes me one. Janet, love, I *promise* you. This could be a gold mine.'

'Why is it always a feast or a famine with you?'

'This is all kosher,' he insisted. 'I'm telling the truth. Why don't you trust me?'

'Because you always let me down.' Her gaze and her tone were both noncommittal. 'Are you intending to stay?'

'No, I've got to get back.'

Janet was brusque. 'Say goodbye to Alan, then. He's got to go back to school. I've got to go back . . . to work.'

Ian had expected a much more cordial reception.

'Is that it?' he said.

'Thanks for the ham and eggs.'

Dick Dobson trudged through the deserted camp with Eric Clayton beside him. Happylands looked miserable. The visitor was intrigued as the project was outlined to him.

'Well, Eric. What do you think?

'All too familiar, isn't it?'

'Certainly is,' said Dick. 'I can smell the cookhouse.'

'I think it's the drains.'

'When can you and your chums make a start?'

'Straight away,' said Eric. 'We can be on this job this afternoon. They'll be only too glad to get stuck in.'

'It's a deal.' Dick gave him some money. 'Fifty pounds cash. No names, no pack drill. When the job's finished, there'll be another hundred. You can divvy it up as you please.'

'Thanks, Dobson,' said Eric, pocketing the notes. 'You're a gent. We've had it hard. You don't know how much this means to me. We won't let you down.'

They parted company and Dick went off to join Lorimer. His boss strolled through the woods in his tweeds with Dick as his gun bearer. They talked about the new labour force.

'You happy with these blokes?' asked Lorimer.

'Old soldiers. Salt of the earth.'

'Why don't they already have jobs?'

'Deasey's problem,' said Dick. 'They can't settle.'

Lorimer scowled. 'Just so long as they don't all want to be in the cabaret at the end of it!'

'I doubt that.'

'Fair enough. One volunteer's worth ten pressed men.' He stopped abruptly and snatched his gun from Dick. 'Oi!'

Lorimer had seen a poacher, crouching in a ditch. The youth was holding a rabbit and debating whether or not to make a run for it. Lorimer made up his mind for him.

'Stand still, laddie, or I'll fill your pants with shot.' He turned to Dick. 'Get a stick and give him a good hiding. Unless he'd rather be dealt with by the local constabulary.'

'Come on, Rudi,' said Dick, leniently. 'It's only a tuppenny bloody rabbit.'

'He's a poacher. Teach him a lesson. Go on, Richard.'

Dick searched for a stick but the boy had other ideas. He flung the rabbit at Lorimer and raced off. Lorimer fired the gun in the air and the shock made the boy trip and twist his ankle. Turning around, he saw Lorimer aiming the gun at him so he got up and limped off. A second barrel was discharged harmlessly into the air. Lorimer tossed the dead rabbit to Dick.

'There you are, Dobbo. Dinner for you and Deasey.'

'You had me worried for a moment,' admitted Dick.

'Think I'd shoot the little sod? Not with a witness.'

Rudi Lorimer marched off with a ripe chuckle.

Ian Deasey would not have believed he could enjoy spending time with his erstwhile colleague, Norman. The Bentley took them into Epping Forest to ensure privacy for their deal. Norman took out some scribbled notes and looked at them.

'It can all go on an I A request,' he said. 'Jack will pass it straight through to Plowman at D D Dispatch. They'll issue a Four-Four-Eight . . . ' He turned a page. 'And with a "Priority" cover, the labour allocation can be added to the normal P C San Assignment. Nowt like an ordered system.'

'No,' said Ian with a grin. 'There isn't, is there?'

'The invoices will just go in with all the other Drainage

and Domestic on the monthlies. Won't even cause a ripple.' He nudged Ian. 'Don't you miss it, eh? The cut and thrust?'

'Hearing you Norman . . . almost.'

'There's just one last "t" to be crossed.'

Ian gave him a fat envelope and Norman examined it.

'There you go, old son,' said Ian. 'I'll dot your "i's" on delivery.'

Ian drove on to make another call. Business could now make way for pleasure. With half a dozen eggs and a shapeless lump of butter, he went up to Hedda's flat and tapped on the door.

'Who's that?' she called out.

'A tall, dark, handsome stranger,' he said.

'That's funny. Sounds just like that berk, Ian Deasey.'

The door opened and he thrust his gift at her.

'Look what I've brought you – food!'

'You really know how to treat a girl,' she said, taking the things across to her little pantry. 'Thank you.'

'Sort of a peace offering,' he said, coming in.

'So?' she was unappeased. 'Where the hell have you been?'

'It's a long story.'

'Just give me the interesting bits.'

'Janet slung me out.'

'Predictably.'

'So I went down to see Dick at this place in the country.'

'Predictably.'

'And I've ended up working for Rudi Lorimer.'

Hedda stared. 'You've *what*!'

'Didn't predict that bit, did you?' he said. 'I'm fixing up a holiday camp for him.'

'Well, thanks for letting me know!' she said. 'I thought we were going to work up an act together.'

'We are, Hedda. When it's finished – the camp – he's giving me and Dick a spot on the variety bill. Lorimer's going for the big names, top acts. Real opportunity.'

'For you, maybe. What about me?'

'You know, he's interested in you, Hedda.'

'Most men are,' she said. 'You're an exception.'

'Listen,' he assured her, 'when the moment's right, I'm sure I can get you taken on there as a singer. Doing your own stuff. I guarantee it.'

'What do I do until then?'

'You've always been good at filling in. Far better than me.' He patted her arm. 'You won't have long to wait.'

'People are always telling me that, Ian.'

It was the best tea they had had for years. Janet, Edith and Alan sat around the table in the kitchenette and licked their lips. Ian's food delivery had been a blessing.

'When's he bringing the next lot?' asked Edith.

'Don't get your hopes up, Mum. You know Ian.'

'True, Janet! Mind you, that was a lovely meal.'

'Dad's going to buy a Bentley,' boasted Alan.

'Yes, love,' said Edith, 'and I'm going to marry the Pope.'

'Well, why shouldn't you?' he said and they giggled. 'Don't laugh at me!'

'We don't mean it, Alan,' said his grandmother. 'Don't spoil it now. We've had a lovely tea, haven't we?'

'Thanks to Dad!'

'All right,' conceded Janet. 'Thanks to your Dad.'

Edith nodded at Alan. 'Shorthouse here says the doctor came round to see you on Saturday.'

'He popped by, yes. Sweet of him, I thought.'

'Very sweet . . . Well, looks like it's back to short rations for a bit.'

'We've managed before, Mum.'

'Well, take my advice,' said Edith with a wink. 'Never say no to a bit extra on the QT – if you can get it.'

'Hear, hear!' said Alan.

The women hooted with laughter. He was baffled.

Rudi Lorimer was astonished at the progress being made on site. It was a hive of activity. The labour force was hard at it and new fixtures and fittings were being unloaded from a lorry. HMS *Amazon* had sunk without trace and Happylands was rising slowly out of the waves. A contented Dick and Ian stood with their boss and surveyed it all. A man went past with a new lavatory pan.

'Careful with that,' said Ian. 'We don't want to end up with a busted flush, do we?'

Lorimer winced. 'I hope you've got some better lines

than that planned for you new act, Ian.'

'Dozens of 'em.' Ian watched the cisterns and basins coming out of the lorry. 'Pity we couldn't get any pastel shades. My man in Walthamstow could only supply white.'

'Our patrons won't be here to worry about colour schemes,' said Lorimer. 'They'll come to spend money.'

'Bless their little wallets!' said Dick.

Lorimer watched Eric Clayton marshalling his men.

'Most satisfactory,' he said. 'Richard, why don't you invite Corporal Clayton and his chums over for a drink this evening? I'll have a barrel of beer sent up to the house.'

'That's jolly generous of you, Rudi.'

'They've earned a reward – and so have you two.'

Dick and Ian gave each other a thumbs-up.

Alan Deasey did not expect his mother to be waiting for him outside school that afternoon. She had a message for him.

'I'm going out this evening,' she said. 'I've been invited to a little get-together with some of the girls from the ATS group. We'll have a lovely time with no daft men around – including you. OK?'

'When will you be back?'

'Not too late. Want to go round to your Gran's?'

'No.'

'Make your own tea, then,' she suggested. 'There's a bit of that ham left. Now, give your mother a kiss.'

Before he could escape, she planted a smacker on his cheek and a few passing classmates jeered at him. As Janet went off down the street, Alan was joined by his friend, Sam.

'Want to come down the canal for an hour?' said Sam.

'Right!'

'Race you!'

They tore off in the direction of the canal. The tow path was slicked with mud from the rain and Alan lost his footing. He dived forward and landed flat out on the ground. His clothes were covered in mud. That, however, was the least of his worries. As he looked up, a car went slowly past in the road. Dr Jeremy Pollock was driving and Janet was beside him, laughing happily and clearly enjoying herself. Alan was shocked. His mother had lied to him about where she was going and with whom. He turned to his friend.

'You carry on, Sam. I'm going home.'

'Mummy's boy all wet?' sneered the other.

'Sod off!'

Rudi Lorimer was so delighted with the way that Happylands was shaping up that he strolled over there alone that evening. With his shotgun under his arm, he gazed at the camp in astonishment. In the shortest possible time, the new workmen had made the place almost habitable. Lorimer blinked then stared again. It *was* inhabited. The travellers who had renovated the place had also moved into it. Their vans and lorries were parked everywhere and lines of washing stretched between the huts.

He was still quivering when Walter Clayton ran over.

'Are you Mr Lorimer?' said the boy, wiping his nose on the back of his sleeve. 'I want to thank you.'

'Who the hell are you?'

'Walter. My Dad's your foreman, Eric Clayton. You been good to us. Giving Dad a job and letting us have this place to live in.' He grinned at Lorimer. 'You're a good bloke.'

'Thanks very much . . . '

'Where're Dick and Ian . . . ?'

It was a long journey to the nursing home but Hedda knew how much it meant to the young airman whom she had met on her first visit. His injuries were healing now and some of the bandages had been removed. Holding his hand, she sat by his bed and talked about her husband. The patient told her his plans for going home to America. She was reluctant to leave.

'I've got to go,' she said, giving him a kiss.

'Yeah, me too. See you in Long Island . . . '

It was evening when she got back to her flat in London and she felt tired. The promise of an early night vanished when she saw a figure curled up on the ground outside her door.

'Where's my Dad?' said Alan Deasey.

'Not here. Did he say that he was?'

'No.'

'So why have you come, poppet?'

'I thought he was lying again.'

'Does your mum know you're here?' He looked shifty and she helped him up. 'Come on in and tell your Auntie

Hedda all about it.' She saw the muddy coat. 'Where've you *been*?'

She cleaned him up, put him to bed and listened to his story. Hedda then slipped out to make a quick phone-call. When she got back, Alan was almost dozing off in her bed.

'I've spoken to your grandma,' she said. 'She's not exactly happy but she's going to tell your Mum that you're all right. In the morning, you go back – OK?' Alan nodded. 'You're a very naughty boy.'

'Don't say that. I do my best.'

'You haven't done too badly,' she said, ruffling his hair. 'It's not every man who's allowed into my bed.'

'Honestly?'

'What are you implying?'

'I don't know.' She chuckled and he was hurt. 'Women are always laughing at me!'

Hedda gave him a soft kiss on the forehead.

'You're just like your Dad . . . '

The party was in full swing at Burwood House. Beer was flowing and spirits were high. Eric Clayton and his men certainly knew how to celebrate. With a captive audience on hand, Deasey and Dobson were soon entertaining the troops. Ian moved on to his celebrated rendering of 'I'll Take You Home Again, Kathleen'.

'The biggest one you've ever seen . . .
A great thick stick of Brighton Rock!
I hope you'll try to understand.
I only tried to wipe it clean,
It went all sticky in my hand.
At least you know where it has been . . . '

He got no further. The door crashed open and Rudi Lorimer burst in to discharge both barrels of his shotgun into the plaster moulding on the ceiling. It snowed.

'Get out!' he yelled. 'Out, the bloody lot of you! Out of my house and out of my holiday camp!'

'What's up, Rudi?' asked Ian.

'These bastards have moved their stinking families into Happylands. They're bloody squatters!'

'Let's not get excited, Mr Lorimer,' said Eric, taking the shotgun from him. 'I'll hang on to this, shall I? We don't want any unpleasantness, do we?'

'Bastard!'

'Listen, chum,' said Eric with dignity. 'I fought for five years for this country. A country where I was born – unlike you! I lost my wife, my business and my bloody house. Why should you be opening a bloody holiday camp when my lad and I are sleeping in the back of a van?'

With the gun under his arm, he led his men out. They laughed at Lorimer and clapped him on the back as they went past. Lorimer turned a glacial stare on to Ian and Dick.

Janet Deasey was glad that she had agreed to spend the evening with Pollock. It gave her a chance to relax with him in a way that was impossible at work. He drove her back to his flat above the surgery and opened a bottle of wine. A pleasant evening soon began to have romantic possibilities. By the time they moved on to the brandy, Pollock had his coat off and Janet was curled up on the sofa with him. Since her husband had walked out on her, Janet felt that she was entitled to some fun elsewhere.

'Had a nice time?' he whispered.

'Lovely, thanks.'

'You sure your boy can manage on his own?'

She turned her face towards him and smiled invitingly. 'He can wait a little longer.'

'I've waited quite a while myself . . . '

Pollock kissed her and Janet responded eagerly.

Ian Deasey and Dick Dobson were in a familiar situation. Yet another of their performances had been wrecked. They had lost the most comfortable berth they had ever found. Just as they were settling in to Burwood House, the bubble had burst. They crept away like beaten dogs.

With nowhere else to go, they thumbed a lift back to London and made their way to Hedda's flat. It was late when they arrived and they climbed the stairs on tiptoe. Dick spoke in a whisper.

'Ian,' he said. 'I'm sorry. Speak to me.'

'It wasn't your fault, Dick. You meant well.'

'What a cock-up!'

'Story of my life,' mused Ian.

'We'll find something.'

'Yeah – but what?'

They reached the door and Ian knocked on it. When there was no answer, he rapped it harder and called in through the keyhole.

'Hello . . . Anybody in?'

They heard footsteps coming and got ready to greet Hedda with their kisses and excuses. But it was Alan who opened the door. Rubbing sleep from his eyes, he stood there in his underpants as if in no way surprised to see them.

'Hello, Dad,' he said. 'Hedda's in bed.'

CHAPTER 14

They were dejected. Life in London was not the joyous existence they had envisaged while they were pipe-dreaming in the desert during the war. Ian Deasey and Dick Dobson were not luxuriating in the flesh-pots of the capital, after all. They were struggling to survive. It seemed as if a glorious future was behind them.

To cheer them up, Hedda Kennedy took them along to the jazz club in Soho that night to hear some hot music in a smoke-filled cavern. There was a hint of danger in the air, and many of the patrons were American servicemen. The place was really swinging.

Ian, Dick and Hedda sat at a table in the corner. The beer might be flat but the atmosphere was electric. All three of them were transfixed by a set that featured a handsome young black saxophonist. Hedda saw with amazement that it was her friend, Oliver, the GI from the US Embassy, who had been so helpful to her in the quest for news about her missing husband. Oliver had a real musical talent and the audience acclaimed it.

'Hot stuff!' said Dick in admiration.

'Fancy another?' asked Ian.

'If we can afford it.'

They rummaged simultaneously in their pockets and brought out a sad collection of copper coins. Hedda sighed.

'You can't afford it,' she said. 'Besides, you've had enough already. Quit while you're losing.'

'There's enough for two halves of mild,' said Ian.

Dick nodded. 'You're on.'

'Then I'm off,' decided Hedda.

Oliver came over to greet her, grinning in welcome.

'Good evening, Mrs Kennedy,' he said, politely.

'Do you know this man?' asked Dick.

'Sort of.'

'Oliver Lee,' introduced the saxophonist. 'I work in the records office at the embassy. I've been helping to trace Mrs Kennedy's husband.'

'Good for you.' Ian shook hands. 'Ian Deasey.'

'Hi.'

'Richard Dobson,' said Dick, rising for a handshake. 'Dick to my friends. Do join us, Oliver. I really loved your set. Bit of Charlie Parker in there, eh?'

'Hey, thanks,' said Oliver. 'You got ears, man.'

'People are always telling me that,' said Dick.

'Can I buy you guys a drink?'

Ian and Dick spoke as one. 'Pint of bitter, please.'

'How about you, Mrs Kennedy?'

'That's really sweet of you, Oliver, but I have to be getting home. Busy day tomorrow – for some of us.'

'Want me to see you home?' said Ian, gallantly.

'You're a real gentleman, Ian, but your place is here. With the nice man who's buying a round.' She moved off. 'Lovely to see you again, Oliver.'

'Night . . . ' He turned to the others. 'Two pints of bitter? Don't go away. I'll be right back.'

'What an obliging fellow!' said Dick.

'Who's Charlie Parker?' wondered Ian.

An hour later, the two of them rolled out into a foggy night in London town. Oliver had obliged by buying a second round of drinks and the mystery of Charlie Parker had been solved. As they walked along the embankment, Dick and Ian felt that they had had a wonderful evening. A bus came along and Dick ran towards the distant bus stop.

'Come on! It's the last one!'

'What are we going to pay the fare with?' The truth stopped Dick in his tracks. 'If we step it out, we'll be home in forty minutes. Walking is good for us.'

'That's what I have against it.' Dick fell in beside him. 'Why don't you sell your bloody motorbike? Might as well. We can't afford to buy any petrol.'

'We *could* afford petrol – if we sold the bike.'

'Brilliant idea!'

'What-ho, Carruthers!'

'What shall we do on the morrow, old fruit?'

'Breakfast at Brown's.'
'Luncheon at L'Escargot.'
'Dinner at the Dorch.'
'See a show.'
'Supper at the Savoy.'
'Sounds super . . . so . . . '
They linked arms and burst spontaneously into song.

'Tight as a drum, never been done . . .
Queen of all the fairies.
Ain't it a pity, she's only one tittie,
To feed the baby on . . . '

Janet Deasey lay in bed with Jeremy Pollock and puffed on a post-coital Woodbine. They had the languid togetherness of lovers. She blew an experimental smoke ring into the air.

'Have you ever been abroad?' she said.

'Malta, if that counts.'

'And before the war?'

'Paris. I was nineteen. A memorable trip. And you?'

'We went to the Isle of Wight once,' said Janet as she exhumed the memory of a grim event. 'On Ian's motorbike. Alan was sick on the ferry – he was only four and had never seen the sea. It rained all weekend.' She stubbed out her cigarette in the ashtray beside her. 'We had a wonderful time.'

'Sounds idyllic.'

'I'd better get back.'

'Must you?' He stroked her arm.

'Yes, Jeremy,' she said with reluctance.

She got out of bed and he admired her lithe, naked body.

'I'll take you home.'

Janet pushed him back into bed and kissed him.

'Best not.'

Dick Dobson's flat was a squalid little room with a sagging brass bedstead in the middle of it. Situated next door to Hedda's flat, it had none of its cosiness and tidiness. Empty beer bottles and saucers full of cigarette ends littered the floor. Dick and Ian were fast asleep in their preferred head-to-toe position when Hedda let herself in.

'God!' she exclaimed. 'This place stinks!

She crossed the room to pull back the curtains and throw up the window. Fresh air brought Ian Deasey awake.

'What?' he muttered.

'This came for you.' She tossed an envelope on the bed.

'What is it?'

'A telegram.'

'What's it say?'

'How do I know? See you later. Work calls . . . '

Hedda went out and slammed the door so hard that the noise even penetrated Dick's consciousness. He stirred.

'Oh! . . . Who was that?'

'Greta Garbo.'

'Not again.'

'I told her you vanted to be alone.'

'Quite right.'

Ian opened the telegram and gaped at its contents.

'Bugger me!' he exclaimed.

'Not until I've had a cup of tea . . . '

Scott and Hodges came out of the lift and walked into the lobby at Broadcasting House. Both were dressed in smart suits but their officer habits had not been discarded. When Scott saw a man peering at the statue and trying to make out its inscription, he was back at once as a second lieutenant.

'Straighten up, that man!'

Dick recognized the voice well enough to ignore it. He turned away from the statue and looked into the smug faces of his two former army colleagues.

'Now,' he said, as if their names eluded him, 'Scott and . . . Hodges, isn't it?'

'And what brings you to BH?' said Hodges.

'A summons from Lord Reith. It seems the BBC is short of original talent. Lot of people using second-hand material.'

Scott ignored the jibe. 'One assumes that your partner in crime lurks somewhere close by.'

'Ian is in the ablutions.'

'Cleaning them?' said Hodges.

'Do give him our fondest regards,' said Scott.

'Of course.' Dick beamed. 'Pip, pip.'

As the two men headed for the exit, the commissionaire opened the door and touched his peaked cap in respect.

'Good morning to you, gentlemen . . . '

'Morning, Martin,' they said in unison.

Ian Deasey arrived in time to witness the departure.

'They're known everywhere, aren't they?'

'So it seems. Why is that?'

'Ah, well, they're officers. Gentleman of breeding . . . '

'And education.'

'So it's only fair. Isn't it?'

'No,' said Dick. 'What did the man at the desk say?'

'Wait.'

'How long?'

'As long as it takes.'

Dick lit up a cigarette and returned to his study of the statue and the inscription chiselled out of the stone. The Latin completely baffled him. Ian translated for him.

'Nation shall speak truth unto nation.'

'How on earth can you read that?' said Dick.

'I had a classical upbringing,' boasted Ian. 'Also, it's written on that card down there.'

Dick chuckled. 'Have we got time for a swift half?'

'No, no. Better not, eh?'

'Why?'

'Because we mustn't foul up again, Dick, old chum. This is our big chance. Summoned to the BBC by telegram.' He tapped his forehead. 'Clear head needed.'

'What about a wet throat?' Dick saw the folly of the idea and crossed with Ian to a seat. 'You're right, partner.'

'Should we run over a bit of stuff?' suggested Ian. 'Just in case? You know.'

'Like what?'

Ian pulled a wad of crumpled paper from his pocket.

'It's just an idea,' he said, weakly.

'When did you do this?'

'Just now – in the toilet.'

Hedda Kennedy had picked up a couple of days' work as a model at a couturier's in Knightsbridge. She came out on to the catwalk with professional *élan* and showed off a bridal outfit in front of the steely eye of a titled lady with a plump and plain daughter at her side. The manager hovered in the background and flapped his wrists.

'This is rather special,' he said, as Hedda twirled. 'And rather expensive. From Paris . . . '

It was rejected at once and Hedda took her fixed smile through the curtains and into the changing room at the back. Various other brides were in various stages of undress. Hedda took a cigarette from another model and puffed gratefully.

'No sale?' said her benefactor.

'They're up from Hereford, dear,' said Hedda. 'Happier in gumboots and something in sacking.'

The manager poked his head through the curtains.

'Oi!' he called. 'What about her going away?'

'Good idea,' agreed Hedda. 'We'll have a whip round.'

'Stop it!' he scolded as they all giggled. 'Is there anything in blue that might do the trick for her?'

'Yes,' said Hedda. 'The crew of HMS *Illustrious*.'

The changing room was in convulsions.

Ian and Dick sat on stools in a studio in the basement of Broadcasting House. The production team watched them through the window of the control box. In charge was Ottie Pond the chain-smoking producer, a middle-aged lady with a severe haircut and a face that could stop Big Ben in mid-strike. Beside her was Komical Keith Koster, the putative star of the show. Koster was a glum northcountryman with a bovine stare. It would be difficult to imagine anyone less like the children of Britain's favourite radio uncle. An engineer manned the panel and a couple of anonymous figures in suits leant against the wall.

Ian and Dick were not happy with the set-up. Used to a live audience, they were uncomfortable performing to a clutch of faces behind a glass panel. It was like entertaining a tank of very large goldfish.

They read through their scripts without enthusiasm.

'Now Nigel,' said Dick, 'Tell me. What is the perpendicular pronoun? Will you?'

'Aye . . . ' said Ian.

'Very good. You're a bright boy.'

'Aye . . . ' Ian looked up. 'This is appalling rubbish.'

Ottie Pond spoke to them by means of talkback.

'Hello, gentlemen,' she said, then turned to the agitated Keith Koster. 'What's that?'

'Morton Stanley!' said Koster. 'Ha! Ye gods!'

The talkback was cut off. Ian and Dick watched a heated row conducted in mime. Koster kept shooting accusing looks in their direction simply because they had once been employed – and sacked – by the infamous Morton Stanley. The producer gained the upper hand and the argument subsided. Talkback allowed her gruff voice to jump out at them.

'Ready?' she said.

'Yes, thank you,' said Ian.

'Good. Mr Deasey, Ian . . . '

'Aye.'

'Will you read Ginger, please? And Mr . . . '

'Dobson, Dick,' he volunteered.

'You be the Professor.'

'Sounds about right.'

'Whenever you're ready,' she said.

'How many more have we got to hear!' moaned Koster before the talkback cut him off.

Ian and Dick clearly had an enemy in the control box. They launched into the script with an air of resignation.

'So, Ginger,' said Dick, 'how's the world been treating you since last week?'

'Badly, Professor.'

'Badly?'

'Sadly.'

'But you're feeling happy now?'

'Madly!

'And you'll sing a song for us?'

'Gladly.'

Over the talkback, Ottie Pond cut them off at the knees.

'Hang on,' she snapped. 'We're not ready for you yet.'

Recriminations were bitter. As Ian tried to tidy up the flat in a manic burst of house-proudery, Dick lay on the bed and smoked a Capstan. Ian was going at full blast.

'That's it,' he said, emptying an ashtray into the waste-paper basket. 'We won't get a second bloody chance. We're on the BBC file now as "Failed". That means rejected. No bloody good.'

'It was a rush audition,' reasoned Dick. 'They didn't hear any of our own stuff . . . Pass me that ashtray, will you?'

'Do you have to smoke all the bloody time?'

'It soothes my nerves.'

'Well, it gets on mine and stinks the bloody place out. How much do you spend on those things?'

'Would you deny me my last remaining pleasure, Deasey?'

'Yes! You deny me most of mine.'

'Do I?' Dick was hurt. 'You were never like this in the army.'

'Wasn't I?'

'No. Boring, maybe – but not insufferable.'

'And you were bone bloody idle. Who was it who spent half the sodding war covering up for you?'

'Covering up what?'

'Your mess.'

'What do you want?' said Dick. 'A medal? The Clean-Kit Cross, perhaps? The Polisher's Star, with bar?'

'I wouldn't mind a bit of recognition, that's all.'

'All right, I recognise you. You're Ian Deasey. The Whining Wonder of Walthamstow. Can I have my ten bob reward now, please?'

'You can have a kick up the arse in a minute.'

'Dear God, it's come to this! Domestic violence.'

Ian howled. 'I can't cope with all this filth!'

'So why don't you go home?' taunted Dick. 'I bet dear little Janet keeps the old prefab as neat as a proverbial pin. All the kit neatly laid out for inspection, seven o'clock sharp, every morning. Alan's shoes highly polished, razor-sharp creases in his underpants, satchel lightly oiled . . . '

'All right, warned Ian. 'Leave it out.'

'I'm glad I'm not married, if that's what it's like.'

'No!' yelled Ian. '*This* is what it's like! We're broke. Out of work. Can't pay the rent. We had a try-out for the bloody BBC and we muffed it. We could have been on radio and instead we're stuck here in this pigsty!'

'So?' Dick was maddeningly calm. 'Are we any worse off than yesterday . . . Anyway, I thought I was rather good.'

'You were bloody awful!' said Ian, hurling the ashtray at him. 'I was bloody awful. The whole bloody thing was bloody awful!'

He stalked off towards the door in a towering rage.

'Off out?' said Dick. 'You couldn't get me a box of Abdullahs, could you?'

Edith Cooper missed nothing. When her daughter called to see her at the shop, she decided it was time to impart some wisdom acquired through long and bitter experience.

'How's the job at the surgery going?' she asked.

'Very well, thanks.'

'I bet the doctor is glad to have you.'

Janet turned away from her to hide a light blush.

'Yes. I work hard for him.'

'Don't work *too* hard,' said Edith. 'Don't expect any more that what you're getting from Jeremy Pollock. He's got a career to think about. A reputation . . . '

'What about Frank Parsons?' retaliated Janet.

'A future . . . '

'We've all got a future, Mum.'

'Have we?' She walked round to face Janet. 'All I'm saying is – enjoy yourself while you've got the chance, but don't expect it to come to any more. Then you won't be disappointed, will you?'

A brooding pause. 'Fair enough.'

Ian Deasey's anger with Dick Dobson had not abated. As he stood with Hedda at the bar in the jazz club that night, Ian glared at the stage where Dick and Oliver were improvising together. Piano and saxophone intertwined beautifully and the lively audience cheered on the jam session.

'Look at him!' said Ian with disgust.

'Stop it,' ordered Hedda. 'Have a drink.'

'Thanks . . . '

Ian wanted to sit in a quiet corner and get slowly drunk but Dick had other ideas. As his session with Oliver came to an end, he invited Ian up on-stage. The audience chanted encouragement. Against his will, Ian joined the two musicians and got a round of applause.

'Good to see you,' said Dick. 'How long, is it?'

'You should know. We were in the army together.'

'That's why we called you Donkey Deasey!'

'And you were known as little Dick Dobson.'

The audience laughed and Ian began to thaw out.

'Happy days!' mused Dick. 'What do you want to do?'

'I'm easy.'

'Easey-Deasey. Take it away!'

Dick launched into an up-tempo rhythm and Oliver picked it up on the saxophone. Ian grabbed a trumpet, pretended to play a few notes then went into an impromptu blues.

'Went out today to see if I could get
A chance of being on the radio set.
Radio people gave me a test,
Said no thanks, but I done my best.'

Hedda was strangely moved. Ian was singing with great feeling then miming hilariously on the trumpet. Dick shouted an interjection and Ian used it to spin off into another verse. The trumpet routine again brought laughs. Another verse was conjured out of thin air.

'I said – not today,
Broadcast blues are driving me insane,
If my blonde baby turns the radio on,
I swear to God I'm going to give her one.'
'You going to give her one?' said Dick.
'You bet!'
'Broadcast blues!' they sang. 'Broadcast blues!'

Ian managed a single discordant note on the trumpet and Dick and Oliver had a musical collision to bring the spot to a cacophonous conclusion. Hedda led the warm applause. Ian and Dick were delighted at their reception but they had no idea how important their little act had been. It was a turning-point for them. A woman stood in the doorway, watching the performance with a new understanding of the talents of the two men, and she clapped with the rest.

It was Ottie Pond.

CHAPTER 15

Against all expectation, they were back in a studio at Broadcasting House. Dick was seated at the piano while Ian rehearsed a script with Komical Keith Koster and his co-star, Nigel, a ventriloquist's dummy with an Eton collar and the distinctive suit. Secure in her control room, Ottie Pond peered through the glass and issued her edicts via talkback.

'Go on,' she said. 'From the top again.'

'Ye gods!' groaned Koster. 'All right. Ready, Ian?'

'Fine, yes. Carry on.'

'Intro!' cued Ottie.

Dick played 'The Sun has Got His Hat On', the theme tune for the programme.

'Standard intro!'

'Welcome to *Radio Playtime*,' said Ian, smiling into the microphone, 'with everyone's favourite uncle, Komical Keith Koster!'

Ottie was curt. 'Applause. Go on.'

'And the incorrigible infant himself,' continued Ian, 'Naughty Nephew Nigel!'

'Applause,' said Ottie. 'Keith.'

'Greetings, giggleboxes!' he said in his flat Northern monotone.

'Laugh. Nigel.'

'Ciao, chucklebunnies,' said the dummy.

'Laugh. Ian.'

Ian read the next deathless line and Dick rolled his eyes heavenwards then clutched desperately for a cigarette.

The Astor Club was a favourite haunt of the Mayfair set and it had the requisite luxury. Booths and alcoves gave comfort and privacy. Chandeliers and marble statuary reinforced the feeling of opulence. Even when it was empty, the club had an air of upholstered exclusivity. Rudi Lorimer was wearing a smart pin-striped suit as he showed off the establishment to Hedda Kennedy. She had told him about Ian and Dick.

'What a pair of clowns!' he said.

'They're not doing so bad,' she argued. 'I wouldn't mind a wireless spot, if I got the offer.'

'You're not built for radio.'

'So what am I built for, Rudi?'

He laughed then directed her gaze around the club.

'Have you ever seen such sumptuous surroundings?'

'A long way from the Blue Parrot Club,' she noted.

'The what?' he said,vaguely. 'Where was that?'

'Come on now, Rudi. You mustn't lose sight of your roots. You began in the dirt.'

'Who cares about that? It's where I'm going to that counts.' He grinned at her. 'And who I'm taking with me.'

She feigned indifference. 'How do you intend getting there and what happens when you arrive?'

'What?'

'I might have travel arrangements of my own.'

'Who with?'

Alan Deasey sat at the upright piano in the living room and picked out a tune with one finger. His mother was within earshot as the boy sang quietly to himself.

'The Grand Old Duke of York,
He had ten thousand men
His case comes up in court next week,
He won't try that again . . . '

'Alan!' she scolded, coming in from the hall.

'I'm practising.'

'Well, you can go and practise washing yourself,' she said, sternly. 'Bath time. And you can wash your mouth out with soap while you're at it.'

'Dad's on the wireless tomorrow night.'

'So I understand.'

'Are you going to listen to him?'

'No.'

'Why not?'

'That's my business.'

'Why not, Mum?' he pressed.

'Don't start, Alan,' she warned. 'Please.'

He resumed his tinkling on the piano and sang again.

'His case comes up in court next week,
He won't try that again.'

Alan ducked as his mother took a playful swipe at him.

'Bath!' she ordered.

Hedda Kennedy stood in front of the mirror in her room and adjusted her tight-fitting evening gown. She looked even more stunning than usual and added a touch of perfume for good measure. Ignoring her, Ian Deasey sat on a chair and studied a radio script, muttering the lines to himself over and over again.

'And today, we're sharing a smile, a song and a splint with the staff and the patients of St Nicholas's Hospital for Sick Children . . . '

Hedda moved a strap on her dress and turned round.

'What do you think of it?'

'Too much padding,' he said, engrossed in his script.

'No, there isn't,' she complained, proud of her full bosom. 'Take a proper look, Ian!'

He glanced up. The satin dress defined her figure beautifully and the plunging neckline stopped within half an inch of indecent exposure. Ian was impressed.

'It's lovely, Hedda. Smashing. Honestly.' He went back to his script. 'Greetings, giggleboxes. Ciao, chucklebunnies.'

'Sure you don't fancy coming for a drink?'

'Better not,' decided Ian. 'I want to work on this. Big day tomorrow. It's got to be dead right.'

'You're word-perfect already. Anyway, it's a *radio* show. You can have the script in front of you.'

'That's not the point, is it?'

'Then what is?'

'I want to make a good impression.'

'Please yourself. I'm off.' She picked up her handbag and moved to the door. 'Where's Dick, anyway?'

'He just popped out to give me an hour's peace. He'll be back any minute now. Dick can help me rehearse.' Ian did not look up as she let herself out. He read his next line with deep solemnity. 'I say – it's time for a song . . . '

The jazz club was a cauldron of noise once again and the patrons listened with foot-tapping approval. Dick sat at a table with Oliver, lit two cigarettes and handed one to his companion.

'Thanks,' said Oliver, inhaling deeply then nodding in appreciation. 'What's in these things, anyway?'

'Only the topmost leaves of the famous Yenidje tobacco. Rolled on the thigh of a young Macedonian Maiden.'

'I'm a Virginia man myself.'

'Really?' said Dick with interest.

'Richmond, born and raised.'

'Nice town?'

'Nice enough.'

'Virginia,' mused Dick. 'Named after the Virgin Queen. As in "Carry me back to Old Virginny . . . " And indeed, "The Blue Ridge Mountains of . . . " '

'Stop it,' said Oliver. 'You're making me homesick.'

They listened to the music for a few minutes and joined in the applause when it stopped. Dick turned back to him.

'You said you had a record of Miff Mole.'

'Miff Mole and his Molers,' confirmed Oliver with a grin. 'Want to come round for an earful of great sound? I'll throw in a quart of bourbon.'

'I'm sorely tempted.'

Oliver leaned forward across the table.

'Listen, Dick. Have to talk to you about something.'

'What?'

'Hedda.'

Edith Cooper clattered away in her kitchen at the rear of the corsetry shop. She was making lunch for herself and her grandson. Alan had just arrived with his mother and he made straight for the wireless to twiddle with the knobs.

'What are you doing?' said Edith.

'Tuning in, Gran.'

'I'll do it for you in a minute.'

'Leave him, Mum,' said Janet, 'or you'll never hear the end of it. Alan knows the frequencies off by heart.'

Edith came out of the kitchen to take a first proper look at her daughter. Janet was wearing a pretty dress with an attractive brooch on the front. Her hair had been home-permed and she had taken extra care with her make-up. Edith guessed at once the reason for it all.

'You look very smart, Janet.'

'Do I?'

'Very smart indeed for . . . what was it?'

'Looking at some lace embroidery.'

'Oh, yes,' said Edith, going along with the excuse. 'Of course. I could do with a couple of pillow cases.'

Squeaks, whines and crackles came from the wireless as Alan fought to tune it in. The women exchanged a knowing look then Janet gave her mother a kiss.

'Cheerio, Alan,' she called.

'Have a nice time,' he said.

'Come away with you, young man,' said Edith, briskly. 'Leave that wireless alone. Your dinner's ready.'

'What is it, Gran?'

'Vinegar sandwiches.'

Janet went out laughing.

Ian Deasey was very angry with himself. Having rehearsed his lines into the small hours, he had fallen into a deep slumber that might have gone on indefinitely if Hedda Kennedy had not roused him out of bed. He was late for the performance of the radio show. Not only was Ian forced into the reckless extravagance of taking a taxi, he was mystified by the absence of Dick Dobson. His flatmate had not come home for the night. Ian was livid.

When the taxi dropped him at Broadcasting House, he ran in through the door and raced down through the corridors. The studio audience for his programme had arrived in force and Ian had to fight his way through masses of children in bandages, plaster casts and wheelchairs. He was handing off yet another nurse when he saw Ottie Pond swimming towards him through the tide of wounded juveniles. Her eyes blazed.

'Where the f . . . udge have you been!' she said, amending the expletive just in time. 'Do you know what time it is, Ian?'

'I overslept,' he apologized. 'Is Dick here?'

'No.'

'Then where is he?'

'You tell me.' She clutched at her hair. 'Keith's going round the bloo . . . lasted bend, as it is. Neither of you here. I thought you and Dick lived together.'

'We do. But he didn't come home last night.'

'Then where in God's name is he?'

Ottie Pond got her answer at once. Dick Dobson himself appeared at the end of the corridor, groping his way towards them and looking as if he was far more sick and sorry for himself than any of the children around him.

Ottie was disgusted. 'Look at the state of him!'

'Morning,' said Dick, bravely. 'I'm fine, really.'

The effort of speaking was like a punch in the stomach to him. Retching wildly, he darted into the cloakroom further up the corridor. The producer was shaking with rage.

'See to him, Ian. For pity's sake!'

Ian jostled his way back through the heavy traffic of injured infants. Sounds of vomiting came from the cloakroom.

'Excuse me, kids!' shouted Ian. 'Let me through. I'm a doctor. This is an emergency.'

One of the doctors accompanying the children looked at him with suspicion, clearly doubting that this maniac in a demob suit was a member of the medical profession. Ian plunged into the cloakroom, where Dick was spewing up with dramatic effect.

'Where the hell have you *been*, Dobson?'

Seeing that his partner was in no position to conduct a sane conversation, he cleaned him up, vented his spleen upon the hapless pianist then dragged him off to the studio. Dick recovered enough to have a brief word in private with Ottie. Her fury calmed at once. Ian wondered what Dick could possibly have said to her. He had poured oil on the troubled waters of a Pond.

Keith Koster was still in turbulent mood. Surrounded by an adoring audience of sick children, he stood on the stage in front of a battery of microphones with Naughty Nephew Nigel on his knee. When Ian half-carried Dick in and lifted him bodily on to the stage, the children's favourite uncle was less than avuncular.

'You're late!' he hissed. 'First time on the air and you show up late. I've been in this business for thirty-two years and I've never been late. Not once. Not ever. Not by a bloody second.'

'Amateurs!' said Nigel. 'Typical.'

'We're sorry,' said Ian, holding Dick upright.

Ottie Pond now intervened to calm her star down.

'Keith,' she beckoned, coming up on-stage.

'What *is* going on, love?' he said, tetchily. 'Why am I being treated like this? Tell me – what is happening?'

'Dick's mother died,' whispered Ottie. 'He shouldn't have come but he's such a trouper. Be kind to him, Keith. On his first day. Help him through it, there's a pet.'

Koster went from indignation to morbid sentimentality but it was Naughty Nephew Nigel who spoke.

'You should have said, old boy.'

'I didn't think of it,' said Dick.

'Good lad!' said Koster.

'He's one of us,' added Nigel.

Dick stared glassily at the dummy. 'Where's the sound coming from?' he said.

'We're on in minute,' warned Ian.

'Good luck!' called Ottie, heading for the control room.

'I've got it,' said Dick, dropping to his knees and peering under Koster's chair. 'It's coming from here.' Ian yanked him up and dragged him to the piano stool but Dick wanted to pass on his discovery. 'He talks through his arse.'

'Shut up, please!' said Ian.

'All right,' agreed Dick before belching loudly.

'By the way,' said Ian. 'I'm sorry. I really am.'

'Are you, love? What about?'

'Your Mum. How did you hear?'

'From my father.'

'When?'

'Nineteen thirty-four, I think . . . '

Ottie Pond's voice exploded out of the control room.

'Are we ready, everybody . . . ?'

Epping Forest was a favourite spot for courting couples now that spring had finally come. Jeremy Pollock had to drive for some while before he found a secluded glade. Janet sat beside him, rehearsing what she was going to say. He was flirting light-heartedly but the outing had a more serious purpose for her.

The car stopped and they began to unload the picnic things from the rear of the car. As Janet laid the tartan rug on the grass, he brought across the sandwiches.

'The perfect spot,' he said. 'Discreet and leafy.'

'Jeremy, I've come to a decision.'

'Oh, yes?'

'I'm getting rid of Ian.'

'When you say getting rid of . . . ?'

'I'm going to divorce him.'

'Murder's less messy,' he quipped.

'I'm serious.'

He did not like the sound of that. 'I see.'

'But that doesn't mean I expect you to . . . '

'To what?'

'To step into his shoes, as it were.'

'I see.' He was relieved.

'I managed as a single woman for four years all through the Blitz – and Alan wetting the bed. I can manage again. I'd rather be on my own than have to be dependent on a man.' She watched for his response. 'One like Ian, anyway.'

But Pollock was no longer listening. He had seen two figures strolling along the path towards them. As Janet bent into the car again, he grabbed her buttocks to shove her out of sight. He was too slow to avoid being spotted himself.

'Jeremy!'

A well-spoken young man bore down on him with his smiling girlfriend. Pollock slammed the door on Janet and covered the rear window so that the newcomers could not see her. Hidden in the car, she could hear every word.

'What a surprise!' said Pollock, uncomfortably. 'How are you, Bransby? Hello, Ruth . . . '

The young couple looked down at the picnic on the rug.

'All alone?' said Ruth.

'Er, yes . . . ' said Pollock.

'Where's your young lady?'

'Which one?'

Bransby Saunders sniggered. 'You haven't changed, you old dog. I say, is that smoked salmon I see down there? So this is what you get up to in your spare time, Jeremy.'

'What?'

'Private practice!'

Ruth recalled a name. 'Annabel, wasn't it?'

'Ah, yes. She's . . . looking at lace embroidery.'

'Make a change from you looking at hers,' said Bransby.

Crouched in the car, Janet was undergoing some swift disenchantment. Promises made to her during intimate moments now took on a different meaning. The two friends clearly knew Jeremy Pollock much better than she did. What really annoyed her was that – while she was locked away – they were now wolfing the picnic that she helped to prepare. Bransby's teasing eventually came round to the subject of marriage.

'Isn't it time you got yourself hitched, Jeremy?' he said. 'What's the matter, not found the right girl?'

'No, not yet.'

'Not for want of trying!'

'You've been through dozens!' said Ruth.

The conversation had exposed Pollock in his true light. When they finally departed, he raced across to let Janet out of the car and heap apologies on her. She was icy.

'You were too ashamed of me even to introduce me.'

'Not at all, Janet. It was just . . . inconvenient.'

'I'm sorry if I constitute an inconvenience!'

'Don't be silly, old girl.' He turned on his charm. 'How are you feeling now, my love?'

'Bloody angry!'

In spite of the last-minute panic, *Radio Playtime* was going down extremely well with the staff and patients of St Nicholas's Hospital for Sick Children. Ian was delivering his lines crisply, Dick was managing to play the piano in tune and Keith Koster was doing his double act with Naughty Nigel. Everything was leaping neatly off the script until they came to the closing section of the show.

The favourite uncle cued in Ian Deasey.

'What do you say, Ginger?'

'I say it's time for a song.'

'Jolly good idea,' said Nigel. 'What about the Eton Boating Song? Always reminds me of the dear old alma mater.'

'Alma who?' said Ian.

'Alma mater, you oik. Latin for Mum's the word!'

The joke was lost on the audience but they tittered obediently. Dick struck up the chords of the Eton Boating Song and the children all looked at the song sheets which had been provided. It was the climax of the show and Ottie Pond was delighted with the way it had all gone. That delight now turned to stark horror.

'Hang on a minute!' yelled Ian, improvising. 'We don't really want to sing that old rubbish, do we?'

Koster gaped and allowed Nigel's head to sag forward.

'I can think of a much better song than that,' said Ian. 'Who knows "Zippedy Doo Dah"?'

Everyone did and a cheer went up from the children. Ian Deasey was a pied piper who could lead them where he wished.

'Music, maestro – please!' called Ian.

Dick played the introduction and Ottie was powerless to stop him. It was a live broadcast and the song was going out to the listening millions. The glowering Keith Koster and the collapsed dummy sat there in mute horror as Ian led the singing and did a funny, arm-flapping dance.

'Zippedy doo dah, zippedy ay!
My, oh my, what a wonderful day!
Plenty of sunshine, heading my way . . .'

When he stuck to the script, Ian was competent. When he took flight in front of the live audience, he was supreme and the children loved him. As the song came to an end, their acclamation roared down the radio waves. The sick children – and the wider radio audience that included a proud Alan Deasey – had no doubt who was the real star.

Ian had triumphed at last.

CHAPTER 16

Reprisals were immediate. Dick and Ian were summoned to Ottie Pond's office to face her across a cluttered desk. They were like truant schoolboys being admonished by a termagant headmistress. Dick was queasy and Ian repentent. Ottie attacked the culprit.

'You're a prat, Ian.'

'You sound like my wife.'

'God forbid!' said Dick.

'And you're no better, Dick.'

'It's true.'

'What you did was highly unprofessional,' said Ottie.

'Yes,' conceded Ian. 'It wasn't particularly comical.'

'Do you want to hear what everybody's favourite uncle had to say about the fiasco?' Ian shook his head. 'Suffice it to say that Naughty Nigel thinks you're a total turd.'

'I see.'

'What happens next?' asked Dick.

'The long and the short of it is that Keith – and Nigel, of course – don't want you on their show.' The two men were shattered. She threw a lifeline. 'Take heart, boys. You're only the latest in a long line of people that Keith – and Nigel, of course – don't want on their show. How d'you think you got the job in the first place?'

'You heard us in that club,' said Ian.

'Whence I had retired to drown my sorrows,' she confessed. 'You represent the last desperate scrapings at the bottom of a very large barrel.'

Dick nodded. 'We failed to justify your confidence.'

'The copyright infringement penalty for 'Zippedy Doo Dah' will be deducted from your salaries.'

'We're being kept on?' said Dick, hopefully.

'On one condition,' she said. 'You have to perform the Act of Contrition. Say you're sorry and beg forgiveness.'

'From Keith?' said Ian.

'And Nigel . . . '

The two men groaned but the gruesome chore could not be avoided. They went off to find the co-stars in their dressing room. Keith Koster was on the verge of tears and Naughty Nigel was lying over a chair like a wet sock. Ian and Dick grovelled before them and the great man wept.

'I don't know what to say to you,' he said. 'I've been in this business for — '

'Thirty-two years,' they prompted together.

' . . . and in all that time I've never been treated the way you treated me in front of that audience. You made me look ridiculous.'

'Mr Koster,' said Ian, 'that wasn't our intention.'

'No,' said Dick. 'We hold you in great esteem, Keith. Awe, even. You and Nigel. I'm not being facetious. You've made him a living person. I saw those kids' faces. He's like a real little lad to them.'

Koster was touched. He sat the dummy on his knee and slipped his hand into the slit at the back.

'He's real to me,' he said. 'What do you say, Nigel?'

'They're both very naughty boys,' said Nigel.

'Well, you're naughty sometimes,' argued Koster. 'Are we going to give them a second chance?'

'I don't know about that.'

'They're new boys, Nigel. They don't know the rules yet. They didn't mean to upset your favourite uncle.'

'Didn't they?' Nigel's head swivelled. 'Are you sure?'

'We didn't mean it, Nigel,' chorused the miscreants.

The dummy bared its false teeth in a hideous grin.

'Tut, tut, tut, tut, tut . . . '

Relations between them had been strained ever since the abortive picnic in Epping Forest. Dr Jeremy Pollock bided his time for the right moment to attempt a reconciliation. Janet Deasey was checking some files in the surgery when moved in on her.

'Still cross with me?'

'What do you think?'

'Look, I've said I'm sorry,' he argued. 'I panicked. What did you expect me to do?'

'Acknowledge my existence.'

'Bransby Saunders is a notorious scandalmonger. We were at medical school together. If he'd caught me having a bit of al fresco with my receptionist, it would have been in the next edition of *The Lancet*. He's a dangerous man.' He moved closer to her. 'I was only protecting you, Janet.'

'Your friend was right about one thing,' she said.

'What's that?'

'It's about time you settled down.'

'Is it? With whom?'

'That's your decision,' she said.

Rehearsals at the Astor Club were tiring and Hedda Kennedy was exhausted by the time that she got back to her flat. All she wanted to do was to flop down on the bed, but it was occupied by Ian Deasey. Perched on the lace coverlet, he was leafing through an official-looking file.

'What are you doing here?' she said.

'Waiting for you.'

'Where's Dick?'

'He went for a haircut and never came back.'

'I see.'

'How's your day been, Hedda?'

'Not bad, if I say so myself. Old Rudi's got a nice set-up at the new club. I trust that you're going to come and lend some moral support.'

'Try stopping us,' he said with forced jollity. 'We'll be there. Wouldn't miss it for the world. Only . . . '

'Only . . . ?'

'I'm not very good at this,' he admitted. 'Come and sit down, sweetheart. I've got something to tell you.'

'You haven't got fired from the BBC, have you?'

'No. Nearly, but not quite.'

'What is it, then?'

'Well, you know Oliver, the black lad. Dick's pal . . . '

'From the American Embassy? I know him well.'

'He called while you were out. Left this for you.' He indicated the file. 'He's found out. About Eddie.'

'Oh, God!' Hedda sank down next to him, looking

shaken and vulnerable. When he put a consoling arm around her, she pulled away. 'What? Tell me, Ian. For God's sake, tell me!'

'He's alive.'

'Thank heaven!' She burst into tears and embraced him. 'Thank you, Ian.' She looked up at him. 'Where is he?'

'He's in Portland, Oregon.'

Alarm showed. 'In hospital? Is he wounded? What?'

'He's on a farm,' said Ian, quietly.

'A farm?'

'Yes.' He broke the news as softly as he could. 'With his wife and their two children. Two little girls.'

'No.' Hedda was aghast.

'Young Oliver took out this file,' said Ian, offering it to her. 'He's not supposed to and he'll be in a lot of trouble if anybody finds out. He thought you ought to know.'

'Why didn't he tell me before?'

'It's not policy, apparently. A lot of them have done the same trick, it seems.'

'Trick?' Hedda was destroyed. 'Some trick!'

Rudi Lorimer was cruising around the Astor Club with a contented smile of his face. The glamorous surroundings had brought in some high-class clientele with expensive tastes. The place was filled with dinner jackets and cocktail dresses. His smile faded when he saw that two of the dinner jackets were occupied by Dick Dobson and Ian Deasey. He went to their table and curled a supercilious lip.

'Ah,' said Dick, 'you've come at last, waiter!'

'What are you two doing here?' hissed Lorimer.

Ian beamed. 'Dying of thirst, at the moment.'

'Could we see the wine list?' asked Dick, grandly.

'There's nothing on it you can afford,' said Lorimer then gaped when Dick offered him two fivers. 'I'll get you a waitress.'

'Can we have a drink first?' joked Ian.

The lights dimmed and the band struck up. A female vocalist in a sequined dress stepped into the spotlight. Lorimer withdrew to the shadows to watch her but it was Ian Deasey who looked on with most interest and compassion.

Hedda Kennedy sang with real heartbreak in her voice.

'That's the way it goes . . . '

Alan Deasey sat with his best friend, Sam Potter, in a little tent in the latter's garden. Sam was dressed in a Boy Scout's uniform and was setting out food on the groundsheet. They were equipped with storm lanterns, primus stove, mess tins and other gear designed for survival in the wilderness. Their one luxury was a Bakelite wireless, the lead from which went snaking up the garden to the house. As Alan gulped down some tea, his friend pointed to the sandwiches.

'Which one?' said Sam. 'Bovril and cheese . . . or cheese and honey?'

'Cheese and honey, please.'

The whole tent shook violently and Sam yelled. The grinning face of his father came in through the tent flap. It was Norman, the rising star of Walthamstow Council.

'Only me,' said Norman, chuckling 'Dib, dib, dib. Not to mention dob, dob, dob.' He looked at the creature comforts set out for the boys. 'You wouldn't be much good up the grey-green Limpopo, would you? . . . You all right, Alan?'

'Yes, thanks, Mr Potter.'

'How's your lovely mum? Still on her own?'

'Yes,' said Alan. 'As far as I know.'

'As far as you know, eh?' Norman cackled. 'That's good, Deasey. You're as comical as your old Dad!'

'Yes, Mr Potter.'

'How about a sandwich, then?' said the interloper, taking one and biting into it. His face turned blue. 'Strewth! What's in this!'

'A secret recipe, Dad,' said Sam.

Norman spat it out. 'Your Mum suggests you use the toilet before you settle down,' he advised.

'I went before. I'll survive.'

'Be it on your own head.'

They waited until they heard his footsteps fade away then switched on the radio. It was a long time before Alan could listen to his father's programme but he wanted to be ready for the big event. He and Sam munched happily away.

Ottie Pond sat in her glass-fronted control box with a couple of engineers. The studio audience of Girl Guides and Boy

Scouts trooped noisily in. As they took their seats, the din was overwhelming. Ottie signalled to Ian and Dick to take up their positions on stage, but the tumult did not die away. Ian waved ineffectually.

'Hello, hello! Settle down now please.' He held up his hands. 'Can we have a bit of hush, boys and girls?'

When the noise continued, Ottie switched on talkback.

'Shut up, the lot of you, or you're out on your arses!'

Her savage request was instantly met. Silence reigned.

'Thank you,' said Ian, taking over. 'Hello, everybody. We'll be starting soon but there are one or two things I have to tell you before we go "on air". So – I'm Ginger and that's the Professor over at the old pianola there . . . ' Dick played a few bars of music. 'Keith and Nigel will be here very soon. Nigel's just finishing his homework . . . '

Ian got a reassuring giggle from some of the younger members of the audience. He glanced at the control unit and got a gesture of encouragement from his producer.

'Thank you,' he continued. 'So the main thing is to keep nice and quiet – except when there's a song or a joke. Then you can sing or laugh, as much as you like. OK?' A murmur of consent. 'And . . . we're going to pretend that we're all camped out under the stars, sitting round the campfire. All right? Good.'

'Stand by!' warned Ottie's voice.

'Here we go, kids,' said Ian. '*The Gang Show.*'

He pulled a face and got them laughing. Komical Keith Koster then made his entry with Naughty Nigel on his arm. There was loud applause. The co-stars took up positions.

'Greetings, giggleboxes!' said Koster.

'Ging gang goolie, girls and boys!' said Nigel.

His jaw jammed in the open position. Koster coped with the crisis neatly by slamming the open mouth shut with his other hand. The kids roared with amusement.

'Steady on, lad,' the uncle said to his nephew.

'Coming on air . . . ' warned Ottie. 'Cue!'

Dick gave Ian a wicked smile then played the theme song. Ian conducted them all in a rousing chorus.

'The sun has got his hat on,
Hip, hip, hip, hip, hooray.

The sun has got his hat on,
And he's coming out to play.'

'Welcome to *Radio Playtime*,' said Ian, 'with everyone's favourite uncle, Komical Keith Koster.'

'Greetings, giggleboxes,' said Koster after the cheer.

'And the incorrigible infant himself . . . ' said Ian.

'Naughty Nephew Nigel!' yelled the audience.

'Ciao, chucklebunnies!'

'And this evening,' said Ian, 'we're deep in the bush. Shepherd's Bush, to be precise.' Jungle sounds played in the background. 'Sitting by the campfire with as jolly a group of Scouts and Guides as ever wiggled a woggle . . . Are you in the Scouts, Nigel, old bean?'

'Catch me sleeping in a tent?' said Nigel. 'Not likely. Out in the open, prey to all manner of wild beasts? No, ta.'

The dummy's jaw stuck open again. Koster forced it shut before shooting a look of panic at his producer. Ottie gave him a thumbs-up. Ian and Dick suppressed giggles.

'Well, what about you, Professor?' asked Ian.

'What about me, Ginger?' said Dick.

'Do you like being in the jungle?'

'Rather . . . '

Koster was due to come back into action but he was now wrestling with his nephew and failing to get the mouth-mechanism to work again. Ottie gave Dick a signal to keep going.

'Rather . . . ' repeated Dick.

'Rather what?' said Ian.

'Rather be at home in bed.'

'Shame on you! I remember a wonderful week with the Third Walthamstow. Deep in the Forest of Epping.'

'What happened?'

As the two of them improvised, Ottie Pond came rushing in to assist Koster to repair the stricken Nigel. Dick took a small spring from his pocket. It had once operated Nigel's mouth-piece.

'It was in the terrible winter of nineteen twenty-two. August Bank Holiday. The snow was four feet deep. I was twelve . . . ' Ian ignored the sounds of the distraught Keith Koster, weeping copiously behind him. 'One of the lads went missing. Mackintosh, his name was. We used to call him Tosher. He'd gone to collect wood for the campfire . . . '

The spring sprung out of Dick's hands and was lost.

'And . . . ?' he asked.

'He never came back,' said Ian. 'We organized search parties. Dark, bitter cold it was. Enough to freeze the ribbons off your garters. Finally, we found him . . . frozen. He'd lost his bearings in the snow.'

'Nasty!' said Dick.

'All blue, he was. I had an old coat of my Dad's so I wrapped him up in it. Saved his life, that coat. And do you know?'

'No. What?'

'I've still got it. Whenever I wear it, I remember that poor frozen Boy Scout. I put on that coat and I think – "Mackintosh!"'

Groans came from the audience, drowning out the anguish of Keith Koster. Dick played a few chords on the piano.

'Well, Professor,' said Ian.

'Yes?'

'After all that, I think it's time for a song . . . '

Alan Deasey and Sam Potter roared with laughter as they listened to their wireless in the tent. Two wellington boots lay beside them. The boys were both quite tipsy.

'Your Dad's brilliant!' said Sam.

'What do you say, Nigel?' mimicked Alan.

'I say it's time for another . . . '

He produced a bottle of beer from inside a boot.

Celebrations were held at the jazz club that night. Ian and Dick had sabotaged the dummy and saved the show. Ottie Pond told them that Komical Keith Koster had fled to his hideaway in Broadstairs to recover from the humiliation. Unaware of their part in his downfall, Koster had praised his colleagues and insisted they do the show in his absence. Ottie downed a whisky and laughed.

'Think you can cope with the Canvey Island Sea Scouts?'

'Aye, aye, sir,' said Dick, saluting.

'Just keep it clean,' warned Ottie.

'You can rely on me,' said Ian.

Oliver joined them at the table to invite Dick to play in a jam session, but the latter suggested they listen to records instead. The two of them went off to Dick's flat with a bottle of bourbon so that the mood of celebration could continue.

The sight of Oliver reminded Ian of the file which the young GI had delivered. While they were all enjoying themselves at the club, Hedda was probably weeping her eyes out at her husband's betrayal. Ian shared one more drink with the delighted Ottie Pond then left.

Bathed in moonlight, Janet Deasey and Jeremy Pollock lay on the bed in his flat. She sat up and stared into infinity.

'Still pensive?' he said.

'Mmmmmm.'

'What do you want me to do?'

'Be quiet.

'What exactly's on your mind?' She remained withdrawn. He looked up at her. 'Clark Gable?'

'No.'

'I know what I'm thinking of.'

'So do I.'

'Good.' He reached out for her.

'Hang on!'

'What sort of talk is that?'

'I'm not sure.'

'Oh' He was peeved. 'Not-sure talk, is it?'

'Sorry.'

'Wake me up when you've made up your mind,' he said. 'If it's a yes vote, that is.'

Janet waited until he was asleep then crept out.

A rueful Hedda Kennedy moved around her flat as Ian watched.

'So you've decided, then?' he said, gently.

'Yup,' she replied. 'God Bless America, I say! Bye-bye Buick, farewell Frigidaire . . . '

She took the photograph of her husband and dropped Eddie into the bedside drawer before closing it for ever.

'So long, Eddie . . . '

'Well,' he said, 'it looks like we're all going to get what

we want, one way or another, doesn't it? . . . What next?'

'You could at least take your coat off.'

'I thought you wanted to go to bed.'

'I do.'

'Oh . . . '

'I just feel like a bit of company for a while.' She slipped off her dressing gown and slid between the sheets. 'If you're not too tired, that is . . . ?'

Ian hesitated for a moment then took off his coat.

'Want me to tell you a story?'

When they finally drifted off, it was in a mood of sweet contentment. She had lost a husband and he had lost a wife but they had at last found each other. Ian Deasey and Hedda Kennedy slept serenely. Adversity had drawn them together.

They were soon ripped untimely from their slumber. Chaos erupted outside on their landing and they staggered to the door to see what was happening. Four burly American Military Policemen were frog-marching a half-naked Oliver downstairs. Two uniformed constables were hauling Dick Dobson out of his flat in his underwear under the eye of Detective-Inspector Wareham.

'What's going on!' said Ian.

'Keep out of this,' said Wareham. 'These two men have committed a very serious offence.'

'What have they done?'

The Inspector looked at Hedda then drew himself up.

'I don't like to say in front of a lady, sir.'

CHAPTER 17

Silhouetted against the wild sky, Hedda Kennedy wore a Wren's uniform and an expression of deep sorrow. She spoke to a handsome man in the uniform of a naval officer.

'I've spent this whole beastly war saying goodbye,' she said wistfully. 'Goodbye to people who never come back. People I love . . . '

'I'll come back, darling,' he said. 'I promise.'

'Then I'll not say goodbye to you. Not ever, ever . . . '

'Cut! print!' called a peremptory voice.

The screen test was over. Hedda looked towards the director for approval he merely gave her formal thanks. Roy was a short, fat, irascible man of middle years with thinning hair and a cynical manner. His scowl changed to a polite smile when he saw Rudi Lorimer striding over to him.

'I thought she was excellent,' said Lorimer.

'Very raw. Pretty, though. Which helps.'

'She'll soon pick up.'

'There's little enough time to shoot the damn thing as it is, Mr Lorimer,' complained Roy, 'without having to give acting lessons to the leading lady.'

'Well, if you don't think you can handle it . . . '

Roy heard the veiled threat from the money man.

'You're right. She'll be fine.'

'Excellent, excellent. I'll tell her.'

Lorimer was soon walking along with Hedda on his arm. She had changed out of uniform and was thrilled with her day at the film studios.

'Don't you worry about a thing, sweetheart,' he said. 'Old Roy's got great confidence in you. He should know.'

'He's made a lot of pictures,' she said.

'Roy knows star quality when he sees it.'

'Thanks for everything, Rudi.'

'My pleasure.' They reached the Bentley. 'Want a lift?'

'Ralph wants to give me a lift in his sports car. He's a wonderful actor. He helped me through that scene.'

'Bit old for the part, though, don't you think?'

'No. Do you?'

'Ralph's in his thirties,' he said. 'It needs to be played like a boy going away to school for the first time. He's both excited and scared. Innocent, vulnerable . . . '

'Virginal?'

'Exactly,' said Lorimer. 'You and he should be like Romeo and Juliet. Two star-crossed lovers . . . '

A pause. 'I wonder how poor Dick is getting on.'

Crumpled, unshaven and thoroughly miserable, Dick Dobson sat in the interview room at the police station. Across a bare table was Detective-Inspector Wareham, who lit a cigarette without offering one to the prisoner. He consulted his pad.

'How long has this sort of thing been going on, Mr Dobson?'

'What sort of thing?'

'The sort of thing you were up to with your little nigger friend. Where'd you start all that, then? Boarding school, was it?'

'No,' said Dick. 'I've never done it before. Never.'

'I see. Moment of weakness, was it?'

'I suppose it was.'

'Followed by a lifetime of regret.' As Dick lowered his head in shame, Wareham pressed home his advantage. 'You do realize that this is a very serious charge? You may be liable – if found guilty – to a term of imprisonment of up to ten years. Corporal Lee is under twenty-one, and black.'

'What's happened to him?' asked Dick.

'On his way home, Mr Dobson. Not exactly to a hero's welcome, I'm afraid. So . . . '

'So what?'

'Just out of interest . . . ' Wareham turned back a few pages in his notepad. 'What can you tell me about Mr Rudi Havel?'

When Hedda Kennedy got back to her flat, she found Ian

Deasey at the dressing-table, writing He rose to give her a welcome kiss. When he tried to embrace her, she held up the letter she had just collected from the hallway below.

'Second post,' she said. 'Your loving wife.'

Ian took the letter and tore it open. She looked at his meagre belongings in the little cardboard box on the bed. He was absorbed in the contents of the letter.

'Did you see Dick at the police station?'

'He needs help. Wants to talk to Lorimer's lawyer.'

'Palliser? What about?'

'He was rather . . . evasive.'

'It's got a bit serious all of a sudden, hasn't it?'

'Certainly has.'

'It's not your fault, Ian,' she cautioned. 'Save your own skin. Don't get involved in other people's problems.'

'I can't help it.'

'Two star-crossed lovers.'

'Who are you on about, Hedda?'

'What a bloody mess!'

Alan Deasey sat in bed that evening and read the letter which his father had sent him. He chuckled quietly at the corny jokes. When he heard his mother coming, he thrust the letter beneath the bedclothes. Janet was surprised to find him in his pyjamas.

'You're in bed early,' she said.

'Yes.'

'Why?'

'Why not?' he said, cheekily.

'I beg your pardon!'

'Nothing. Sorry.'

'I should think so,' she said, reproachfully. 'You're not too big for a good hiding, you know.'

'No, Mum.'

She sat on the bed and softened, pushing his hair back from his eyes and thinking how like his father he looked.

'I don't mean it, Alan.'

'Thought you were going out again. With the doctor.'

'Change of plan,' she said. 'I'm tired.'

'Dad wants to see you.'

'I want to see your dad,' she admitted.

'Is he coming home?'

'No, Alan. I'm afraid he isn't.'

'Why not?'

Janet shrugged. 'Because, in the long run, I think we're all happier as we are.'

'No,' he said, angrily. 'You're jealous because he's got on the radio and he's a big success and you didn't want him to be. You just wanted him to do a boring old job for the council.'

'I wanted a bit more than that, Alan.'

'I want him home with us.'

Janet pursed her lips and nodded sadly.

'Me, too. But he'd rather be with someone else.'

The last time he had seen Ottie Pond, they were celebrating together at the jazz club in Soho. As he faced the producer now, across a desk in her office at Broadcasting House, the mood was very different. Ian Deasey was being interrogated.

'How long have you known him?' she said.

'Four years. We were in the army together.'

'And you never suspected?'

'Of course not.'

'But you got closer to him than anyone.'

'There was a bloody war on,' snapped Ian. 'Anyway, what difference does it make?'

'Quite a lot, in this case.'

'It's nobody's business but his.'

'Grow up, Ian,' said Ottie, levelly. 'It's everybody's business now. A man is judged by the company he keeps. This is a kid's programme. What else can I do?'

'I don't know. What do you usually do, Ottie? You look as if you know more about it than I do.' A glint came into her eye. 'What's your secret, eh?'

'Discretion, Ian, which is the better part of valour. I admire your sticking by Dick, and I feel sorry for him, but he's out of the game now, permanently.' She spelled it out for him. 'The BBC is the BBC. Forget Dick. Think of yourself. You've got to decide what *you're* going to do.'

Ian was seething at the injustice of it all.

'It just isn't . . . right,' he said.

'I know but that's the way it is.'

'Thank you.'

☆ ☆ ☆

Edith Cooper took her daughter into the kitchen at the rear of the shop for a liberal dose of tea and sympathy. Her advice was, as ever, thoroughly practical.

'Nobody in the world would blame you, love,' she said.

'Alan does.'

'Well he would, wouldn't he?'

'It's not his fault, poor mite.'

'And it's not yours,' said Edith, firmly. 'You're only doing what any woman would do in your position.'

'Am I?' Janet was uncertain.

'Yes. Don't feel guilty. Men never bloody do. They don't have to carry the can, do they? Sod 'em all!'

'Including Frank Parsons?'

Edith bridled. 'You leave Frank Parsons out of this,' she said, tartly. 'Just concentrate on your own life, on what you want to do with it, and don't worry about anybody else. That's my advice.'

'All right,' agreed Janet. 'Just tell me, Mum . . . You and Frank. How long has it being going on?'

'Five years. Every Tuesday and Friday. Regular as clockwork.' Edith met her eye. 'Happy?'

'Are *you*?'

'Yes, thank you, and so is Frank. We're not doing any harm to anybody, are we?'

'What about his wife?'

'Tuesday and Friday nights, Rose has her Bible classes,' said Edith, briskly. 'She found God during the black-out, bless her, and Frank found me – so everybody can have a little of what they fancy. That's all that makes the world go round, isn't it?'

'I suppose so, when you put it like that.'

'Exactly. You can't change nature . . . ' Her daughter suddenly shook with mirth. 'What are you laughing at?'

'You're no better than you should be, Mother!'

'Neither are you.'

'Well, it's obviously the way I was brought up.'

Edith joined in the laughter then made more tea.

A relieved Dick Dobson came out of the police station with Ian Deasey. Being in custody had reminded him too much of the army and he was glad to be a free man again.

'Thanks, Ian,' he said. 'Thanks a hell of a lot.'

'You should thank Hedda. She spoke to Lorimer, he spoke to Palliser and that little so-and-so got you bailed for fifty quid. All Hedda's doing.'

'Bless her little cotton socks!'

'Rudi's going to want his fifty quid back,' said Ian.

'He's going to want a damn sight more than that, old son,' said Dick ruefully.

A grubby little man in a raincoat accosted them.

'Spare me a moment, gents?' he asked. '*Daily Sketch.*'

'No, thanks,' said Dick. 'Excuse us.'

'I understand you gentlemen work for the BBC.'

'Not any more,' said Ian.

'Ah, you are Mr Dobson's "partner", then?' said the man with an insinuating snigger.

'Piss off!' said Dick.

'Temper, temper! Please. I'm only doing my job.' He took out a pad. 'So you have both now left the BBC's employ?'

'Leave us alone,' said Ian, angrily. 'What's the matter with you?'

'What's the matter with *you* is more the questions.'

Dick tried the punch the man but Ian restrained him.

'Leave him, Dick. He's not worth it . . . Let's go home.'

'Revolting little animal!' said Dick.

The man sniggered. 'Look who's talking!'

Janet Deasey had spent a great deal of time thinking about her mother's advice but it still did not sit easily with her. At the surgery that morning, she was making an inventory of medical equipment when Jeremy Pollock cornered her.

'You missed a good evening last night,' he said.

'Did I?'

'Bit of Tallis, Byrd . . . and Palestrina, your favourite.'

'Don't tease me, Jeremy.'

'I'm not teasing. I wanted you at the concert.'

'Good job I stayed in,' she said. 'Alan's acting up.'

'There's nothing wrong with that boy that a good hiding wouldn't cure!'

'There's nothing wrong with my son that having a father around wouldn't cure.'

'Amounts to the same thing, doesn't it?'

'If you say so.'

'I do,' he said. 'It's only because he hears Ian on the wireless, isn't it? He thinks it's all terribly glamorous, no doubt. You can't expect him to understand about parental responsibility, can you?'

'No . . . ' She gritted her teeth.

'Thinks the world owes him a living, that's the trouble with your husband.'

'All right, Jeremy,don't keep on.'

'Well, what are you going to do about it?' he demanded. 'You've got to make your mind up, Janet.'

'I have,' she said, coolly.

'Oh.'

Ian Deasey had been cut adrift once more and there was no land in sight. He had already lost his wife, his son and his house. He had now lost his job at the BBC and all prospects of ever regaining it. Worst of all, he had lost his partner. Dick's relationship with Oliver had not only severed the Deasey-Dobson double-act, it could bring a lot of unsavoury publicity for Ian himself. It would be a case of guilt by association. To spare a loyal friend more embarrassment, Dick Dobson had left London. He needed time to recover.

Hedda was still intermittently sharing her bed with Ian but her success only accentuated his own failures. Not only had she landed the part in the film, she now had a regular and well-paid spot as a vocalist at Lorimer's night-club. Ian was once more on the outside, looking wistfully in at showbiz like a child in the Bisto advertisement.

Depressed and aimless, he agreed to the meeting which his wife had sought in her letter. They chose a neutral venue in central London. Ian waited in the lounge of the hotel in his creased demob suit. When Janet arrived, she was wearing a smart new outfit that made him blink. He stood up from his seat and beckoned her over with a tentative wave.

'Hello,' he said.

'Hello, Ian.'

He wanted to give her a kiss of welcome but the table and the weeks of estrangement stood between them. They sat down. He ran an appreciative eye over here.

'You look really good.'

'You look a mess, frankly.'

'Yes, well . . . '

Janet handed him a folded copy of the *Daily Sketch.* He glanced at the article about Dick and winced. The reporter had pilloried both of them. Janet was wounded.

'Thanks very much!' she said with heavy sarcasm. 'This is just what Alan and I needed. I was going to see if we could sort things out. That's why I wanted to meet. But not now. That article changes everything.'

Ian was too deflated to reply. A waitress arrived.

'Can I help you?'

'Yes, please,' said Ian. 'What would you like, love?' His wife looked coldly at him. 'Two coffees, then, please.'

'OK.' The waitress walked off.

'I'll tell you what I really want,' said Janet, leaning across to him. 'A formal separation.'

He was rocked. 'I see.'

'Well?'

'What can I say?'

'Sorry, perhaps?'

'You know I'm sorry. Very sorry.'

'So am I.'

'How's the boy?'

'Oh, he's all right,' she said. 'He thinks you're a hero. He wanted to know if you could do *Radio Playtime* from his school. That was before this nice little piece about you in the paper, of course.' She searched in her handbag. 'He's written you a letter.' She handed him a grubby envelope. 'Here it is. From your son.'

He took it from her and stared at it blankly. The meeting with Janet was not turning out as he had hoped. He began to see things from her point of view and quailed.

'Well?' she prodded. 'Aren't you going to read it?' A longer pause. 'Do you want me to tell him what's happened?'

'How can you?'

'No idea but I'd rather he heard it from me first. I don't want him reading about his father in the *Sketch.*'

'Tell him I love him,' said Ian.

'What about me?'

The question hung in the air like an accusation. Before he could even begin to answer it, the waitress returned with a tray and unloaded the cups on to the table.

'Two coffees. Anything else?'

'I don't think so,' said Janet. 'I'm not staying long.'

Marshall Gould welcomed him with the weary air of a man who had been through the situation many times with many clients. The reviving sherry was dispensed in his office while Ian gazed at the photographs on the walls and wondered how those smiling faces had made a success of such a cruel profession. Gould sipped his drink before clicking his tongue.

'Dear me!' he said. 'How are the mighty fallen!'

'Things could be worse,' said Ian.

'That's the spirit!' The agent slapped his desk with a palm. 'Put it in perspective. After all, what's happened? Your wife's divorcing you, the BBC has kicked you out and your partner's been caught in bed with a black GI. Makes me realize what a sheltered life I've led.' He saw off the rest of his sherry. 'Whatever became of Miss Kennedy?'

'She's got a part in a film with Ken Hawkes.'

'Right, then. That takes care of her.'

'Hedda deserves it.'

'I'm sure she does, Ian. But what do you deserve?'

'Not all this shit!'

'How true, dear boy. What next, though? What next?'

'I hear that Morton Stanley is setting up another touring show,' said Ian, hopefully. '*Morton's Music Hall Memories*. Could you wangle me in there?'

'Be serious!' said the agent. 'By the way, you're going to change your name to Livingstone, aren't you?'

'What for?'

'You can't go about as Deasey any more, can you?'

'Why not? It's my real name.'

'I didn't think you'd made it up.' He became serious. 'Listen, Ian, you've made a reputation for yourself but I don't think it's quite the one you wanted. Deasey and Dobson – the Performing Poofters!'

Ian was insulted. 'I'm a married man!' he urged.

'Only just. Anyway, that's not the point. You're his partner. Tarred with the same brush. A man is judged by the company he keeps.'

'That's what Ottie Pond said.'

'She should know!'

'What am I going to call myself, then?'

Marshall Gould gave the matter considerable thought.

'How about Lucky?' he suggested.

As soon as Janet Deasey got home to the prefab, she knew that she was too late. Her son was sitting at the table in the kitchenette with a torn copy of the *Daily Sketch* lying in front of him. News which should have been broken tactfully to him had been thrust sadistically under his nose. Tears were streaming down his face as he stared at the article.

'How was school today?' she whispered.

'Rotten.'

She tried to put her arms around him to comfort him but he pulled away. The father whom he idolized had been derided in a national newspaper. The hero of *Radio Playtime* was now an unemployed entertainer caught up in a scandal.

'Oh, lovey . . . ' said Janet.

'Sam said Dad's a pansy – so I must be one.'

'Of course you're not.'

'Are you sure?'

'Don't be silly. That's daft.'

'Why? What's it mean?' he pressed. 'Tell me!

She took a deep breath. 'Your Dad's friend from the army . . . he's been a very bad man.'

'But Dad hasn't, has he?'

'No.'

'Dad's not . . . like that.'

'You know he isn't.'

Alan stared at her. 'It's not why you sent him away?'

'No.'

Her firm answer reassured him slightly until he glanced down at the newspaper again. Tears threatened once more.

'I can't go back to school. They all laugh at me.'

'Oh,God!' she sighed. 'It's not your fault, is it?'

She snatched up the newspaper and screwed it up before hurling it with contempt into the bin. When she came back to Alan, he let her cuddle him in her arms. They needed each other more than ever now.

'Don't worry, love,' said Janet. 'They'll soon forget it. It'll pass . . . like everything else.'

CHAPTER 18

He was still fast asleep when Hedda Kennedy burst into the flat and crossed to the bed. She tore back the blankets.

'Wakey-wakey! Come on, Ian! Up!'

'What?' He opened an eye. 'Where've you been?'

'I worked late,' she said. 'Spent the night at Rudi's. He's got a spare room.' She unzipped her evening dress and stepped out of it before putting it on a hanger. 'Hope you didn't wait up for me, darling.'

'I tried.' He got the other eye open and watched her select some clothes from the wardrobe. 'What are you doing now?'

'Getting dressed. Filming starts at nine. Hurry up!'

'Why?' said Ian. 'I'm not going anywhere.'

'Yes, you are. I managed to persuade Roy to let you be in one of the scenes today.'

'Doing what?'

'Earning three quid,' she said, putting on her blouse. 'What's the matter with you? Move!'

'I haven't shaved.'

'You don't need to. You look perfect as you are.' She reached for a skirt. 'But bring your best bib and tucker. We're going on to a party afterwards.'

'Oh, no,' he said. 'I don't want to go to a party.'

'How else will you meet people?'

'I don't want to meet people.'

Hedda looked across at him with irritation.

'That's your trouble, Ian . . . Now, let's roll!'

At the end of the working day, Janet Deasey packed all of her things into the bag she had brought. It was time to move on. She took one last look around the surgery to see if there was anything she had forgotten.

Dr Jeremy Pollock watched her with regret.

'You don't have to leave, Janet,' he argued.

'No,' she said. 'On the other hand, I think I should.'

'Why? This is silly.'

'Is it?'

'Give me one good reason to resign from this job.'

'You.'

'Janet!'

'Want another reason? Me.'

'But we got on so well together.'

'That's why I have to go.'

She lifted the heavy bag and moved off. He stopped her.

'If there's anything I can do, Janet. Anything . . . '

'You could give me a lift home with this lot.'

'Ah, well,' he said, evasively. 'Not now, I'm afraid. Old Wakeley's asked me to cover him. Daren't leave the surgery.'

'Never mind. I can manage.'

As Janet opened the door, a smiling Annabel bounced in.

'Hello, Janet,' she said. 'Just off? Jeremy's taking me to the pictures this evening.' She gave him a warm kiss. 'Am I early, darling?'

'A bit,' he confessed.

'Have fun,' said Janet, wryly.

'Cheerio,' he croaked.

She closed the door of the surgery hard behind her.

Ian Deasey was less than ecstatic about his debut in films. After four years as a soldier, sweating it out in the blazing desert, he was now in the navy, freezing in the ice-cold North Atlantic. The armed forces were never kind to him. Ian was cast as a member of a crew whose boat had been torpedoed. As they clung to the life-raft, their spirits were kept up by their captain, the star of the film and an emblem of British pluck. Ian's role consisted of one line but it involved spending an inordinate amount of time in a tank of water that had been set up in the studio. After an hour of wallowing about in the freezing, urine-enriched sea, he was feeling as if he really had been torpedoed.

Rudi Lorimer sauntered across the studio towards him.

'How's it going, then, Deasey?' he said.

'Very well, thanks. Bit parky.'

'How's Richard?'

'Gone away for a bit. Before the trial.'

'Give him a message from me.'

'Now?' said Ian. 'I'm rather busy at the moment.'

'Tell him that I wish to see him. And warn him to keep his mouth shut – at all costs. All right?'

Ian nodded and watched Lorimer walk away to slip an arm around Hedda. They had come to watch the shooting of the final sequence of the film. Technicians climbed everywhere. Final adjustments were made to cameras, lights and sound equipment. A machine was switched on and the waves began to roll with venomous force. The director came across to the tank to give his instructions. Ian was starting to turn blue with cold.

'Right,' said Roy, bossily. 'Let's knock this off, shall we? Now, then, what's-your-name . . . '

'Ian,' said Ian.

'You've been in the water for hours.'

'I certainly have!'

'You're exhausted.'

'Yes.'

'And you're absolutely frozen.'

'I am, yes.'

'Good,' said Roy. 'OK, everybody! Let's do it!'

His film crew spoke out in rapid succession.

'Turn over!'

'Speed!'

'Seventy-seven. Take one!'

'Wait for it,' said Roy, 'You're losing consciousness. You can't hang on any longer. It's the end. And . . . action!'

The cameras rolled and Ian delivered his one line.

'I can't feel my legs!'

He drowned like Ophelia. It was the real thing.

'Cut. Print. Fine.' Roy was very satisfied.

Ian resurfaced in time to see Lorimer leading Hedda away with his arm around her shoulders. She took a last look over her shoulder then kissed Lorimer and went off with him.

Ian murmured his line and sank beneath the waves again.

The party was held at a superb mansion just outside London and upper echelons of the film world had arrived in Bentleys and Rolls Royces. Tuxedos and cocktail dresses fluttered like butterflies around the lavish buffet and an orchestra played a medley of favourites in the background. Liveried flunkeys poured champagne the moment they saw a half-empty glass. It was a glittering occasion.

Hedda Kennedy took to it as if her whole life had been a rehearsal for this moment. Looking svelte and glamorous, she glided across the room and waved to her numerous admirers. When she saw Lorimer, she went across for a kiss and a dose of his smoothest flattery. Lorimer's smile congealed when Ian Deasey trotted over to them in a blotchy dinner jacket.

'I wasn't expecting to see you here, Ian,' he said.

'He didn't want to come,' said Hedda. 'I twisted his arm.'

'Really? I must try that some time.'

'Nice party,' said Ian.

'Until you arrived . . . '

Roy came over to heap more praise on Hedda and ignored Ian completely. She was a star now and he was very much a nonentity. As the director swept her away to meet some of his cronies, Ian was left alone with the frowning Lorimer. His old boss did not mince his words.

'What the hell are you doing here, Ian?'

'I'm with Hedda.'

'Why? Do you think she needs you?' He hammered home the message. 'She's in a different league from you now. Hedda is flying while you stay on the ground.' He took a glass of champagne off a passing tray. 'If you want to do something useful for once, go and fetch Dobson back to the fold.'

'Why?' said Ian, defiantly. 'Why should I?'

'Because I ask you to. It's for his own good.'

'And yours, presumably.'

'And Hedda's, in that case.'

'I see.'

'I don't think you do,' said Lorimer, darkly. 'Just do as you're told and everything will be hunky-dory, I promise you.'

'What do you take me for?' said Ian, scornfully.

'What did you take Dick for?'

Lorimer turned away and let the question bury itself like a knife in Ian's chest. It had been a big mistake to come to the party. He was totally out of place. There was nobody to talk to and nothing to be gained. Ken Hawkes, the star of the film, was telling an interminable anecdote to a circle of adoring and sycophantic fans. Their artificial laughter caught Ian on a raw nerve. He spotted Hedda on the edge of the group and made his way across to her but Lorimer got there first and slipped a proprietary arm around her.

Ian made a few vain attempts to attract her attention but Hedda seemed to ignore him. He felt hurt and let down. It was the social equivalent of being in a tank of freezing water. It was time to sink again. Ian finished his champagne then put the glass on a table as he walked towards the exit.

Hedda saw him go and thought about calling after him but she turned back instead. The dazzling world of film was more exciting than the hand-to-mouth existence she had shared with Ian Deasey. Rudi Lorimer observed it all with quiet satisfaction.

It was a long drive up to Warwickshire and the motorbike complained and rattled all the way. Ian was glad to turn into the drive of the house. It was a magnificent building, a huge, rambling stately home with a vast expanse of parkland all around it. Dick had been unduly modest about his background. Ian had always been given the impression that his friend came from a prosperous family but he had no idea that they lived on this scale. Was it possible that Dick's father might even be titled?

He drew up in front of the building and took directions from a housemaid. Master Dick, it appeared, was in the grounds somewhere. Ian went tramping off in his motorbike gear. When he finally located his friend, Dick was chopping wood in a glade. Wearing rustic flannels, he swung the axe hard.

'That's a sight for sore eyes!'

'Deasey! What in God's name are you doing here?'

'I've come to see you, mate,' said Ian, wearily. 'Been on the road since five o'clock this morning, but it was worth it to see you doing some bloody work for a change.'

'What's happened?'

'Quite a lot, all in all.'

'Pull up a log.'

'Thanks.' Ian settled himself on a fallen elm and unbuttoned his coat. He took out a tobacco tin and began to roll himself a cigarette. 'You rolling your own now?'

'Tricky to find Sullivan Powell's up here.'

'I suppose so.'

Dick waited until the cigarette was rolled and lit.

'So . . . ?'

'Rudi Lorimer wants to talk to you.'

'You mean Rudi Havel.' said Dick bitterly. 'I bet he does!'

'What's it all about?'

'What do you think? The police have got a file on him as long as your arm. But they can't make anything stick because he's always had a mug like me between him and the law.'

'He's going to get you off, isn't he?'

'So he says.' Dick was sceptical. 'Inspector Wareham claims he can get me off as well – provided I drop dear old Rudi in the brown stuff. I don't believe either of them.'

'I see your point.'

'What do you think I should do, Ian? You've never steered me in the wrong direction, have you, old chum?'

'Yes, I have. Every time.'

Dick laughed. 'God bless you, Deasey!'

'Go to America,' advised Ian.

'What – jump bail?'

'Why not? Lorimer's not short of fifty quid. He'll have got a good deal, and I'm sure it's better than Wormwood Scrubs.'

'True . . . '

'And Oliver's there.' Dick looked at him shrewdly but he met his gaze. 'He probably needs a mate just now.'

Dick nodded and took him by the arm to help him up.

'Come and meet my Dad.'

Ian was embarrassed. 'I'm not dressed for it.'

'Yes, you are. It's this way . . . '

Dick led him off through the bushes. Ian was surprised. Instead of making for the house, his guide took him off in the opposite direction. They eventually came to a covert where a tall, thin man in his sixties was tending some game birds in their cages. He had close-cropped, iron-grey hair and the face of a man who spent most of his time outdoors. Luke Dobbs was wearing a rather tattered set of tweeds. Ian decided that he was an eccentric member of the nobility, who preferred to dress in this extraordinary fashion.

Dick introduced the two of them. They shook hands.

'I'm very pleased to meet you, Mr Deasey,' said the older man, warmly. 'I'm very grateful for the way that you've stood by my son. I truly am. I mean that.'

'Dad knows what's happened,' said Dick.

'Dick and I were best mates right through the war, Mr Dobbs,' said Ian, loyally. 'He's a good bloke.'

'Aye. I think so.' Luke fed grain to the birds.

'What is all this?'

'Dad's the gamekeeper,' admitted Dick.

The truth was out at last. Instead of being the son of a wealthy landowner, Dick Dobson – or Dobbs – was simply a gamekeeper's lad. Ian had been misled by him for years but he did not feel hurt. He offered his own credentials.

'My Dad was a carpenter,' he said.

'You never told me, Ian.'

'Nothing wrong with that,' said Luke Dobbs, emptying the bag of feed. 'Joseph was a carpenter, wasn't he? . . . Fetch me another bag, will you, son?'

'Right,' said Dick and went off towards a little shed.

'Forgive my asking,' said Luke. 'Are you one?'

'A carpenter?'

'One of them, I mean?'

'No.' Ian almost blushed.

'Fair enough.'

'What are those birds?'

'Pheasant.'

'What are they for?'

'Shooting, you daft sod!' Luke chuckled. 'I look after 'em. Feed 'em up, make sure they're nice and fit and healthy. So that – when the time comes – His Lordship can shoot the buggers.'

'Seems a bit of a waste of time, doesn't it?'

'Aye, lad.'

'Do some of them get away?'

'Oh, aye,' said Luke. 'Some of 'em get between the guns, like you and Dick did, thank heaven. I'd rather have him home as he is than a dead hero.'

Dick brought the feed. 'How are the little 'uns?'

'They'll be ready when their time comes, son.'

'They shall not grow old, as we that are left shall grow

old, eh, Deasey?' He turned to his father. 'I'm going back to London with Ian.'

'Oh, yes. How long for?'

'I don't know, Dad.'

The old man continued to feed his birds in silence.

The first thing that Janet Deasey saw when she walked into the ATS Garage was the sight of Annabel's plump behind. Her friend was looking under the bonnet of Tillie, the oldest and most cantankerous of the ambulances. Hearing the approach of feet, Annabel brought an oil-stained face out.

'Just passing,' said Janet.

'Get away! You miss it.'

'I suppose I do in a way. What's wrong with Tillie?'

'Fuel pump,' said Annabel, wiping her hands on a rag. 'She's getting a bit past it, old thing. Wants to be put out to grass. Don't we all!'

'How long are you staying?'

'I don't know.'

'Had any other offers?'

'Yes,' said Annabel. 'One, as a matter of fact.'

'Jeremy?'

Annabel nodded, uncertain how the news would go down.

'Good for you!' said Janet, pleasantly.

'You mean that?'

'I do.'

'I finally pinned Jeremy down.' She giggled. 'What are you going to do, Jan?'

'Move on. I might have a go at teaching. Nursery school, probably. What do you think, Annabel?'

'I think it's a smashing idea.' She slammed down the bonnet of the ambulance. 'That's your lot, Tillie. From now on, you're on your own.' Janet winced at the phrase. 'Let's finish off the medicinal gin, shall we, Jan?'

'Why not?'

They piled happily into the rear of the vehicle.

Dick Dobson sat for the last time on the bed in his flat. Dressed for travel, he had all his worldly possessions packed into the two suitcases beside him. There was a coded knock on the door then Ian Deasey came breezing in.

'There you are,' he said, handing over some travel documents. 'Not the Queen Mary, maybe, but . . . '

'How did you fix it?'

'Ask no questions and be told no lies.'

'Where's Hedda?'

'Keeping Rudi Lorimer occupied for us.'

'Havel.'

'Come again?'

'His real name's Havel,' said Dick. 'And he's guilty of many an evil deed, Ian.'

'Such as?'

'Never you mind, Corporal Deasey.' He shook his head sadly. 'I'd like to have said a proper cheerio to Hedda.'

'She won't be back in time.'

'You sound like you're trying to get rid of me.'

'I am. As soon as possible. So sod off.'

'If that's the way you feel . . . '

'You know how I feel.'

Dick smiled. 'Give us a lift to the station.'

'I can't, I'm afraid,' said Ian. 'Don't ask why. I just can't. All right? There's plenty of buses.'

'I'll miss you, Ian.'

'As long as you don't miss the boat.'

'I won't . . . '

They looked at each other then embraced warmly.

'Goodbye, Dick . . . '

'Ian . . .

The traveller departed with his suitcases and Ian felt a lump in his throat. He did not dare to look out of the window when he heard the door to the street open and close. Ian sat in a chair and looked around the flat at mementoes of happier days. Time passed as he went off into a reverie. He was brought back to reality by the apperance of Hedda in a smart new dress. Ian stood up quickly.

'I wasn't expecting you.'

'Where's Dick?'

'He's gone.'

'Where?'

'A long way away,' he said. 'Where he's safe from Rudi Lorimer, or Havel, or whatever his real name is. And safe from the police and the newspapers and everybody else.'

'What about you?' she asked, solicitously.

'And what about my fifty pounds bail money?' said Lorimer as he stepped in off the landing.

'Look on it as insurance,' said Ian.

'I look on it as a bloody cheek.'

'I couldn't care less, to be honest with you.'

'Where's he gone?' asked Lorimer.

'New York.'

'Who paid for that?'

'I did.'

Lorimer went off into a peal of laughter.

'Greater love hath no mug . . . '

Ian was about to throw him out when Hedda intervened.

'Rudi was going to pay, Ian. He had the same idea.'

'I bet he did!'

'It's the truth.' Lorimer took out a wad of notes and offered them to him. 'Here. Take it, Ian. Go with him. Start a new life – a new act – on Broadway. There's nothing much left for you here, is there?'

Ian looked at Hedda. Her sad smile was answer enough.

'No, there's not a lot,' he agreed, 'but you can keep your money. I'll pay my own way, thank you.'

'Bon voyage, then!' Lorimer took Hedda by the arm. 'Come on, sweetheart,' he said. ' Let's get your things out of the flat . . . '

Reading a book about how to bring up children made Janet Deasey even more dispirited. She seemed to have got nothing right. Alan contradicted her sense of failure by bringing a tray of tea into the living room and setting it down beside her on the occasional table.

'Here we are,' he said.

'That's very sweet of you, Alan.'

'You sit there, Mum. I'm going to look after you.'

'That sounds good.'

He poured the tea, added milk then handed it proudly to her. Janet tasted it and smiled in approval. Alan sat opposite her. He was in an inquisitive mood.

'Mum?'

'What?'

'Are you wearing a corset?'

'No, I am not!' she said, choking on her next mouthful of tea. 'Why ever do you ask that?'

'I was talking to Gran.'

'And she thinks I need one, does she?'

'No,' said Alan. 'She says that women wear them to make men look at them.'

'Why would I want men looking at me?'

'Don't they?'

'Not any more.'

'Good.' He relaxed. 'You've got me, anyway.'

'That's quite true.' There was a long pause while she sipped some more tea and prepared herself. 'Alan . . . '

'Yes?'

'I'm sorry about your father.'

'Why?'

'I'm afraid I made a bit of a mess of things,' she admitted. 'When he first came home, I suppose I wanted things to be the same as they'd been before, except I was different. When he started to do different things, I wouldn't let him. You can't do that, Alan. You can't expect people to be what they're not. You have to love them for what they are.'

'That's what I think,' he said, sagely.

'Good.'

'What about me?'

'What about you?'

'What am I?'

'A twerp.' They laughed.

'But you love me, don't you?'

'Come here, twerp.'

She put her cup aside and he gave her a warm hug.

'I wish Dad would come back,' he said, wistfully. 'We could have another go, couldn't we?'

'One twerp is enough.'

'Not really.

'No,' she agreed. 'Not really.'

'Where is he, anyway?'

'God knows!'

The truck rumbled to a halt at the end of the road and Ian Deasey jumped off the tailboard with a battered suitcase. He called his thanks, slapped the side of the vehicle then waved to the driver as it pulled away. Walking slowly towards the prefab, he rehearsed his speech.

'Janet. I'm sorry. I've been a total twerp. I've now got no job, no money and no motorbike, 'cos I sold it to buy Dick a ticket to sail to America – to be with his boyfriend when he gets put of prison.' He amended the last line to soften its impact. 'To buy Dick a ticket to go to America. I'm willing to have another go if you and Alan are willing to have me back.'

He reached the house and paused to tidy himself up a little. The rest of his speech took him up the path.

'I don't think I can go back to the council. I think I can get a job writing for the woman I met at the BBC.' He made another swift correction. 'For the *producer* I met at the BBC. I really want to try to make it work. This is where I belong.'

He was standing outside his front door. He knocked.

'This is where I belong and . . . '

Janet opened the door at once. Alan stood beside her.

' . . . I love you,' said Ian.

'Dad!'

'And you, Alan.'

Janet threw her arms around him and pulled him inside.

'Welcome home!' she said.

Ian came up for air from a flurry of kisses.

'I had a speech prepared . . . '